MÉTIS

Mixed Blood Stories

MÉTIS

Mixed Blood Stories

Lynn Ponton

SUNSTONE
PRESS

SANTA FE

Sunstone books may be purchased for educational, business, or sales promotional use.
For information please write: Special Markets Department, Sunstone Press,
P.O. Box 2321, Santa Fe, New Mexico 87504-2321.

Book and Cover design ❖ Vicki Ahl
Body typeface ❖ Palatino ❖ Display typeface ❖ Bernard Modern
Printed on acid free paper

Library of Congress Cataloging-in-Publication Data

Ponton, Lynn E.
  Métis : mixed blood stories / by Lynn Ponton.
    p. cm.
  ISBN 978-0-86534-791-5 (softcover : alk. paper)
  1. Métis--Fiction. 2. Métis youth--Fiction. 3. Adolescence--Fiction.
  4. Racially mixed people--Fiction. I. Title.
  PS3616.O62M47 2010
  813'.6--dc22
                              2010038915

Published in

WWW.SUNSTONEPRESS.COM
SUNSTONE PRESS / POST OFFICE BOX 2321 / SANTA FE, NM 87504-2321 /USA
(505) 988-4418 / ORDERS ONLY (800) 243-5644 / FAX (505) 988-1025

**To Sarah and Anne
and in memory of Aurelie**

Acknowledgments

I am deeply in debt to my father for sharing with me his spirit for living. Without him, there would have been no dreams to write. I am also grateful to my mother for instilling in me a respect for schedules. Without her, this book would not have been written.

I thank the members of my family, especially my brother and my daughters, Sarah and Annie, for inspiring me. I thank my uncle Leon Ponton for sharing his knowledge of Red River, Manitoba, and Ashkum, Illinois.

Many have helped with this book, among them Amy Wilner, Kathryn Higgins, Lindsay Kuntz, Katie Chase, Cecile Hitchcock, Dana Goldstein, Tamar Shukakidze, Charlotte Dick, Jim Lees, Madeline Meyer, Sam Judice, Andrew Haber, Alison Owings, Henrietta Leonard, Alan Skolnikoff, Victor Bonfilio, Owen Renik, Marlene Mills, Pat Holt, Stella Le Fevre, Julia Archer, Suzanne Musho, Barbara Loos-Chintz, James Anthony, Virginia Anthony, Peter Anthony, Nancy Bush, Larry Brown, John Boone, Alicia Guttman, Steven Zimmerman, Mardi Horowitz, Ruth Noel, Jack O'Brien, Ira Steiman, Nancy Bush, Sylvine Jerome, Nick Weiss, Aurelie François, and Peter Handel.

I am grateful to the Canadian Studies program at the University of California at Berkeley for reading and discussing this manuscript, especially J. Barry Gurdin, PhD and Professors Tom Barnes, Rick Rhodes, Nelson Graburn, and Rita Ross.

I am indebted to the Métis poet Randy Lundy for his generosity in granting permission to include his work.

I thank Lawrence Bark and Norman Fleury of the Manitoba Métis Federation for their assistance. Dr. Phil Katz in Winnipeg encouraged my early interest in this work. I also thank Fred Shore at the University of Manitoba for corresponding with me on important topics related to this work.

I have attempted to be as accurate as possible about the Métis,
yet this is most definitely a work of fiction.

Cast of Characters

*A*naquad – lover of Elisabeth, father of Annie

*A*ngeline Kirouac – matriarch of this Métis family, mother of Joe, grandmother of Gilles

*A*nnie – daughter of Elisabeth and Anaquad, granddaughter of Gilles

*E*lisabeth – daughter of Gilles, mother of Annie, granddaughter of Joe

*G*illes – son of Joe, grandson of Angeline and Louie Riel, father of Elisabeth, grandfather of Annie

*J*ean Kirouac – father of Angeline, Red Otter, and He Who Moves With the West Wind, husband of Strong Wind

*L*eon Beaucoeur – husband of Angeline

*L*ouie Riel – lover of Angeline, father of Joe, Métis leader

*M*arc – brother to Elisabeth, son of Gilles, uncle of Annie

*M*arie-Thérèse – aunt of Gilles

*R*ed Otter – uncle to Gilles, brother to Angeline, son of Strong Wind and Jean Kirouac

*S*trong Wind (*Ni maw maw*) – mother of Angeline, Red Otter, and He Who Moves With the West Wind, wife of Jean Kirouac

Timeline

1844 – Louie Riel's birth

1855 – Angeline's birth

1869 – Le soulevement (The Birth) of Manitoba: Angeline, Riel, and other Métis flee to the U.S.

1876 – Joseph's birth

1885 – Death of Louie Riel by hanging in Regina, Canada

1908 – Gilles's birth

1951 – Elisabeth's birth

1968 – Chicago convention and Dean Johnson's death

1973 – Annie's birth

Contents

"Li Bon Jeu la direksyoon miyinawn, itayha chimiyouitayhtamak,
li shmaen chee oushtawyawk pour la Nawsyoon
dee Michif ota dans not Piyee."

Dear God, Help the Métis to work together utilizing our
Elders as teachers and preparing our youth for the future.

—Métis Prayer

Prologue – In the Snow

*A*ngeline Kirouac stepped outside the door of her Western Illinois farmhouse and looked across the stubbled cornfield. Far beyond the farm, at the horizon near the distant White Oak Creek, she thought she saw a dark curl of smoke. It could be the train. She felt for the lump of the watch on her hip but did not look at it. Leon had left her his pocket timepiece for this day. She had accepted it but would not need it; she would follow the hour by looking at the light in the sky. She would not miss this train. From the pale sun she saw that she had enough time to pick the winter onions hidden under the snow and simmer them with the dried corn to finish making the chowder for dinner. Gilles would be here by then. She felt for the paper telegram, next to Leon's watch in her hip pocket, and pulled it out one more time. GILLES BEAUCOEUR, WARD OF THE STATE, WILL BE DELIVERED TO HIS GRANDPARENTS LEON BEAUCOEUR AND ANGELINE KIROUAC ON THE AFTERNOON OF MARCH 3RD, 1924 BY THE CONDUCTOR OF THE NORTHWESTERN TRAIN, SAINT LOUIS LINE, ASHKOMB JUNCTION PULL STOP, EXPECTED ARRIVAL TIME 1:40. JOHN McDERMOTT, SOUTHSIDE ORPHANAGE, CITY OF CHICAGO, DIRECTOR OF INDIAN AFFAIRS.

Angeline could not read the telegram, her own English being the spoken word, but she had memorized the message after Leon read it to her and kept the telegram in her coat pocket. She would meet the train at the Ashkomb pull stop. Leon would not. He was in Springfield at the state assembly. He had wanted to send a telegram saying they would be unable to get there, but she had stopped him, insisting that she would.

When the sweet, slightly musty smell of the winter onions filled the house, Angeline decided it was time to check again. She stood on her front porch and saw a dark gray ribbon waving in the sky. Maybe. Then she saw the smoke. The train was winding its way through the cornfields, towards the train station. Her eyes still on the smoke-stream, Angeline plucked off her apron, grabbed her deerskin jacket, and quickly stepped into her snowshoes, strapping them on with well-practiced motions. She picked up the slender wooden poles resting in the snowdrifts by her porch, then remembered the snowshoes for Gilles. They were there at her feet in a small carrying pack she had woven from rawhide the day before. She hoisted it onto her back and started out, stepping slowly at first, the wet spring snow sticking to the webs of her snowshoes. Gradually her powerful movements took over and, breathing faster, she thrust herself across the field, racing the train to the junction. This was a race that she knew she would win. She would arrive at the junction before Gilles. She already could see him sitting alone in her cabin later that day staring out at the fields. Like her, he kept others at a distance, his spirit hidden.

As Angeline plodded through the snow, she recalled how she had not wanted to come to Illinois from Canada as a girl, but there had been no choice. She believed that Gilles didn't wish for it either, a farm where he would be living with his grandparents. He stayed for only a short time last time, two years ago. Now he was sixteen. She wondered if Mr. John McDermott, Director of the Southside Orphanage of the City of Chicago, had told Gilles about the only other option, a reservation school. Would he tell a sixteen-year-old how people were treated in a place like that?

Angeline knew Gilles would want to stay in Chicago and keep looking for his father. He would not want to live on a farm with two old people. He was not alone with that feeling. Angeline thought about traveling to Chicago to search for Joe. She hadn't felt old starting out across the field, but her muscles were suffering now, her knees aching with each step.

She was breathing hard, panting hot and wet. The soggy snow still clung to her shoes, and her legs were heavy as sweat dripped down her body. She wanted to take her jacket off, but it was starting to snow and the wind was blowing—large uneven flakes coming at a sharp angle. Thirsty, she opened her mouth and the wind filled it with crystal powder. She tasted it now—spring snow—sweet to welcome her grandson. Snow continued to blow into her face, crusting over her eyebrows, turning them from dark brown to ivory. Some of it melted and ran into her eyes. She did not care what Leon said, that this boy would never stick, that he was just like Joe, his father. She also knew what he thought, "Just like your people . . . Ange, better that this kid go to the reservation now, anywhere away from here." Angeline had spent years trying to discover why Leon felt this way. Was it the old struggle about Joe, or the way Leon cut everything Indian except her out of his life?

Last time Gilles visited at fourteen he had met that grain seller. Two days later he was gone. She was pretty sure that Joe was the reason and wondered how long it had taken Gilles to find him—Joe, her dark-eyed son who loved wine too much, until he switched to the smooth warm whiskey that stole the soul of her people.

She remembered the first time she saw her own father drink alcohol. They were at a Red River jigging party. He downed the homemade wine in fast, big gulps. Not long after, he fell in a pile at her feet. Only twelve years old, she sat holding his head and watching him, only the whites of his eyes visible through his half-closed lids. He hadn't had a lot—one, maybe two glasses. Leon could consume that much and nothing would happen. She had tried alcohol once, too, one of Leon's French wines, a smooth drink that tasted like the wild grape tea her mother made in the fall—sweet and tart at the same time. It had flooded her body with strange feelings. She hadn't fallen into a pile like her father but instead lay on the cold floor, trapped by a frightening vision. An old woman was crying, holding a carrying basket that looked like it held a baby. She thought it was her grandmother. The woman was walking through a forest for a long time before she came to a large lake covered with ice. Sitting down by the shore, the woman began to chant, louder and louder. A powerful wind began and the baby flew to the other side of the lake, but the woman was left behind. Only days after the dream, a train arrived in Red River bringing carloads of hidden cargo. When its doors opened, an army of men in red coats had spilled out. She and her grandmother had witnessed it—the army had been sent by les organistes of Toronto to kill her family.

Not long after, Angeline and a group of others, including Leon, left Red River, Canada. They walked across a sloping plain covered with drifting snow, then through a dense forest. They crossed a great lake. They were walking through her dream. Angeline believed that her drink of that sweet, tart wine had sparked the vision that led to this future. After that, she knew that her dreams were powerful. And she also had her reasons for not drinking wine.

The train was approaching the edge of the long cornfield. She felt herself slowing down, thirsty. She opened her mouth again, but she couldn't catch enough snow to wet her tongue. The storm had stopped except for a few flakes lazily floating to the ground. Now she could not only see the train, but also hear the loud grinding noises from its engine.

Angeline made it to the junction moments ahead of the train and hunched over, breathing hard. When she looked up, she was caught in the train's shadow, light grey smoke seeping into steam clouds. A hand reached out and held her sweating shoulder—a hand and a voice saying, "Are you Angeline Kirouac?" She guessed it was the conductor, although she could not see his face, smoke filling her black eyes. She nodded at the face that she could not see and tried to talk, finally able to say the words, "I am."

A figure hidden behind the conductor was pushed toward her, the only passenger. She couldn't see his face, either, but this had to be Gilles. Although still young, he was already tall, a head above the conductor. His skinny shoulders stooped slightly in the shadows. Angeline felt his presence more than she saw him. She wanted to say something to welcome him but could not. Other words from other places filled her—tawnshi kiya, the greeting of her mother's people. She did not think he would understand.

Finally she was able to speak in English. "Gilles, come with me. Move back from the train." After she spoke, the conductor stepped up into the car and with an ear-piercing whistle the train departed, heaving coal dust in all directions, as it again began winding its way across the snowdrift-covered fields.

Annie – 1989

Totem Dance

Walking along the edge of a grass meadow
the yellow cat spied the green-eyed girl first.

"Dance with me, California child,
daughter of Métis, Assiniboine, and Cree,
don't leave me here with the wildflowers."

Keeping her eyes on him,
Annie did not flinch
when he arched his long neck and flexed his golden back
for her Weston camera.

Cl . . . click
I am your partner for this set, mountain cat,
she whispered as she crawled closer
bringing his shaking whiskers into focus.

Cl . . . click
I am Tiger Girl,
named by my mother's father
on the morning of my birth.

Cl . . . click
I slide my feet and flick my hair in rhythm with yours
so that I can join with you forever
in an interlocking F stop.

With her third click
the cat lunged into the air, swinging its tail in Annie's face
before it dropped to the earth and
disappeared in the grass.

                                        —Lynn Ponton

A Call

I am awakened by an early telephone call from Dad's doctor. He tells me that Dad fell down the stairs last night. My father is feeling "Okay," but has decided to drive himself to the hospital for a check-up. Almost unheard of, the doctor saw him immediately and ordered a CAT scan. That's why he is calling me. At first, I can't hear what he says but, finally, I do. "Moth-eaten lesions were seen on the scan." I have to ask him to repeat it twice. Lesions on the brain . . . why are they there? He tells me they will have to order more tests. He doesn't know what it means, but I do. The blood for the transfusion during Dad's heart valve repair was tainted. I fly to Chicago immediately, leaving Annie alone in San Francisco.

Dad is sitting alone in the hospital room when I walk in. He doesn't say anything. I pull a chair close to his bed and sniff the faint odor of chlorine in his hair. Good, he is still swimming. Unable to speak, I open my suitcase and hand him a couple photos of Annie in her field hockey uniform and a packet of her poems, which I find resting on the dream catcher in my suitcase. She must have sneaked them in. Dad pulls a pair of worn glasses from his deer-leather case and begins to read one of them. He is reading out loud when the doctor comes in. I give the doctor my chair and stand beside my father. For a long time, no one says anything. Finally, after several minutes, my father speaks. "So this is how it is."

His arms locked in front of his chest, the doctor seems to have forgotten why we are there. When Dad speaks, the doctor shivers a little and then talks quickly . . . virus, immunity, heart surgery, infected transfusion . . . repeating certain words over and over . . . but, he never quite says the word. If I weren't searching for it, I wouldn't have any idea what he is talking about. Medical men.

On and on . . . the doc is still shivering and I am worried that he will never say
it and that I will have to.

"AIDS." It is my father who finally says it. "I believe you are trying to
tell me that I have AIDS. . . ." He then mumbles something in Métis. I lean
closer and ask what he means. "Bad blood," he tells me. "I have bad blood now."
                                                                    —Elisabeth

*F*ear. Anger. Guilt. Mom telephones me from O'Hare airport to
let me know that she is okay. She doesn't want to talk. She says she will
call again from the hospital. Not good. Shit, I knew that when she flew
to Chicago only two hours after talking to one of those dumb doctors.
Even though I was half-awake when he called, I could tell that she was
scared, twisting the split-ends of her hair into these little brown braids.
And she was using this know-it-all attitude, the pseudo-calm veneer that
moms who are doctors practice with their patients and try to use on their
kids when things are not really all right. She thinks it's reassuring, but
it's not. No . . . well, that's not exactly true. Sometimes it is, but this
morning it wasn't. I could see that she was cracking around the edges.
When she spilled a bunch of make-up in her rollerboard suitcase, I told
her, "Mom, you wear it, not spill it." She didn't even laugh. Then she was
just throwing all this junk in on top of it. So, I said, "Look, I'll pack it for
you. Go . . . handle the phones . . . reservation, Supershuttle, you're really
good at that." (She is not, but I let her think that today.) Then, I turned
the suitcase upside down and held it by its plastic wheels, dumping stuff
onto the floor, and I saw why it wasn't fitting. Wedged in the bottom
were her medical bag and some tan leather thing covered with pine
needles and tiny beads smelling like a health store. Way at the bottom,
I recognized the large feathered dream catcher I had made in the sixth
grade, spreading its rawhide spider web on her lingerie. That old thing.
I didn't realize she still had it.

I'm trying to fit all her junk in, stuffing her socks and underwear into her boots—why is she even taking the heavy things—and unwrinkling her gray crepe power suit that she absolutely never wears. It's good for talking to doctors, she says. Yeah, right, I'll believe that when I see it. Underneath her suit, my hand knocks something heavy. A massive dark green book lying face-up. The cover print is small, hard to read: *The Human Immunodeficiency Virus and Its Pathogenesis: Treatment and Prevention*. Mom is looking out our window now, trying to convince Supershuttle that they need to pick her up immediately. She is not watching me so I reach for the book and page through it. . . *AIDS in Central Africa . . . The San Francisco Experience . . .* what is this doing in here? I have stuffed it under her folded suit by the time she turns around to thank me. I'm thinking fast now—that seven am phone call from Chicago that woke us up. Just what was she saying on the phone? Something high-tech medical, not HIV, but some kind of test.

Suddenly I see this picture of Grandpa Gilles sitting in some hospital bed, waiting. I want to ask her, scream at her, *Does he have AIDS, Mom? Does Grandpa have AIDS?* But I don't. I zip close her rollerboard. Everything fits in it now, even my dream catcher. Supershuttle is on the way.

Doctor-mom style, she starts telling me what to do. . . *be sure to take out the recycling, eat the food in the fridge, don't let it spoil, don't let the car run on empty* (my bad habit, the reason we don't have enough gas to get to the airport now). Sure, anything you say, Mom (that's weird for me). The whole time, I keep thinking, *AIDS, Grandpa's got AIDS*. I feel like my face has turned ghosty, but Mom doesn't notice anything, or acts like she doesn't. I carry her rollerboard down to the street while tightly screwing in one of the little wheels that's wobbly. I can tell she is really out of it. I want to say, Mom, look at me. I'm scared, too. But I don't. She hands me a hundred-dollar bill like it was a twenty. I take it and hug her really hard. The shuttle comes.

When I go back upstairs, I close the door to my room and turn up my stereo loud (really loud). At first I think that I'm turning it up because no one is here to yell at me (freedom). Then it happens. I start crying. Adults don't realize that a lot of kids play music loud so that they can do stuff that nobody hears. (Forget adults not knowing that, I hadn't realized that before today.) I want to scream, but I can't get the sound loud enough for that. I turn the music up to ten. My ears are throbbing, but I still can't scream. After doing this for an hour, I decide to call a friend. I need to talk to my best friend Maya.

I call. She doesn't answer. I call her again and again. That's why you have best friends. When you have to talk, they have to listen. All my friends tell me I'm a good listener. Well, today I need someone. Where is Maya? Finally she picks up.

"Hey, Annie, What's up?"

Suddenly, I don't know what to say. I don't have to say much of anything. She does it all.

"Are you okay? You don't seem okay," Maya asked.

"Well . . . I don't know. I'm fine . . ." I waffle.

"You don't sound fine. . . . your voice sounds funny, hoarse."

"I have a cold."

"You didn't have a cold when I borrowed the history homework from you last night. Why didn't you come to school today?"

"My mom had to leave town."

"So . . . you're planning a party?"

"No, Maya, no party."

"Where did she go?"

"Chicago."

"Chicago, huh. Why?"

I don't answer her.

"Why? Look, Annie you gotta talk."

Silence.

"Annie, talk to me."

I take a deep breath. "My grandpa has AIDS." I almost choke on the last word.

"AIDS . . ." Now her voice sounds hoarse. I can barely hear it. She doesn't answer for a long time.

Finally she says, "How did he get it?"

"I don't know."

She doesn't let me get away with that. "Look, Annie, what do you think?"

I don't know what to tell her. . . . grandfathers and AIDS, shared needles and unprotected sex—it doesn't make sense. I talk to her for about half an hour longer, telling her about a backpacking trip that Grandpa and I made in Yosemite that summer. But then I want to hang up. I still can't stop thinking. . . . *how did he get it?* I risk the low gas tank and drive straight to the main library. There's a reason for all those stupid research projects they have you do in high school. I will find it. The cause, I mean. I search for hours, and I find a lot of causes for HIV . . . the H's . . . homosexuality, Haiti, heroin, hemophilia. Seeing them in a list like that, I remember hearing about them in some lecture in school. . . . I hadn't paid any attention to it. It hadn't seemed important.

The Next Day

I spend the night in the hospital, sleeping on a couch crafted for family members, which lies at the foot of my father's hospital bed. When I awake he is singing. . . . Tawnshi kiya . . . the song of Angeline. I want to join in, but hold back, trying to memorize his voice. Sensing that I woke up, he begins to talk.

"They came last night, Elisabeth . . . lots of them. They had taken the path. I was with them."

Who came? What path? I feel myself losing my tentative hold on reality. Usually Dad's faith reassures me. What is going on today? He is still humming. I sit up so I can see his face. His eyes are closed.

"Dad, I'm so scared."

"I am too, Elisabeth."

"Then how can you act so calm?"

"I have no choice. This is my way now."

I feel like I don't have a choice here, either. I want to be strong for him, for me. "Who were they, Dad?"

"They were dead. . . . they were alive. They had feelings. . . . they were numb. I was among them and I was not."

Dad has always been so clear. I know that he is trying now, but it isn't registering. "They were spirits?"

"I don't know, Elisabeth. . . . maybe."

"What about you, Dad? How are you feeling?"

"Like they're taking me in, Elisabeth."

Later that day, before we leave the hospital, Dad speaks about his grandmother Angeline and her death. She took the path. And she had the dreams.

Knowing that she has gone before him gives him courage. It gives me courage, too. I call Annie and tell her that her grandfather has AIDS. She tells me that she already knows.

—Elisabeth

I am parked by the curb, waiting at the San Francisco airport for Mom and Grandpa. I called and the plane is on time. I'm not. Usually, I'm late. Today, however, I'm early. I flip through all the radio stations. Nothing sounds good. Paula Abdul's *Straight Up* is playing, but I'm really listening to my own thoughts. Mom said Grandpa is dealing really well with it. He wants to come for a visit—an extended visit, whatever that means. They're talking about a road trip somewhere, and they want me to go with them. Road trips are something that you do with your friends. Drive all night. Go to places like Reno and Las Vegas. Get a fake ID and go to bars. Mom's idea of a road trip is not like that. She likes to camp and hike. Once she even got me to backpack, but only once. It is not exciting, even though she thinks it's just thrilling. I know that she's doing this one for Grandpa, so I'll go, too, even if there aren't showers and I have to sit in the backseat the whole time.

An airport policeman keeps trying to get me to move. I have waited more than the time allowed—ten minutes—and they still haven't showed up. He has a loud voice, and he's using a megaphone. I decide to get out of the car so he can see me when I talk to him. It usually increases my chances not to leave. It works again. I'm good at debate . . . the soft type of debate where I convince the policeman that it's to his benefit to let me stay. I see that he's looking at me, and why not? I am dressed for the occasion—jeans that fit perfectly, a tight red t-shirt and a black leather jacket. I think that I look the age of my fake ID—twenty-one. But I don't show him that one. He spends a long time looking at my driver's license. I think he is memorizing my address. When he asks me how often I drive to the airport, I know he's gonna let me stay.

I recognize that I'm slightly freaked about this policeman because of what's been happening since Mom's been gone. She left me in charge and I've really fucked up. It was Maya's idea, last night I went over to her place to sleep when I couldn't stop crying after I got a letter from my dad. Some dad—thinks we can have a relationship now that I'm an adult, well almost. Maya convinced me (she really didn't have to try hard) that we should go down to Larkin Street and give out condoms to kids living on the street. She told me that we'd be safe (her cousin Vic would drive us), no problem. Yeah, right, three am on Larkin Street with Maya and her cousin, Big Vic—big problem. First she and Vic got some weed to help them handle how depressing it is down there. Then after we gave out condoms we ended up going to an all-night party in an empty apartment. When I woke up, Vic was sleeping on top of me. And I still don't know what happened. I don't want to ask him. How could I be so fucking stupid? I know how I could be so stupid—I didn't want to go back home alone. I wanna talk to Mom, but I can't. She's got more than enough to deal with.

I see them coming toward me now. Carrying two old leather suitcases, Grandpa walks in front of my mom with a backpack hooked over his shoulders. He is wearing his airforce aviators, and his skin has turned a deep brown like he's been on a long vacation. I can see he is style-conscious, like me. People say we look alike, too—tall, with long, straight brown hair. When he hugs me I notice he's only about five inches taller than me now, but you never know—I'm still hoping to grow a few more inches. Mom looks tired, with violet circles under her eyes. They are wrestling over the suitcases—who's going to lift them into the trunk. Does having AIDS mean that he can't lift those suitcases? He still looks a lot stronger than Mom, even though she swims all the time. *C'mon, Mom. Let him do it. Let him lift them himself. Don't worry so much.* Finally, she gives in, and he hoists the bags into the trunk. I can tell from the way he hauls them that they are heavy. . . . just what did he bring? He shoves his old canvas backpack on top of the bags, and I can see his metal tent poles sticking out, his blanket bedroll and sleeping bag neatly attached by bungee cords. No hotels for him.

The spidery dream catcher that I made in sixth grade is now sewn into the flap of his pack, and its crow feathers shine as he pushes it into the trunk. It seems almost magic. It's weird to think that I created it—just some random school project—we were supposed to make something that was valued by ancestors. I asked Mom for ideas and she didn't have any, but then she started crying when I gave it to her. She thinks I don't notice, but I see a lot of her projects—those trips to the reservations, how she keeps trying to save those Native American kids. Do all kid doctors do that? She doesn't talk about a whole lot of it, so I have to guess. I'm good at guessing—I guessed that she would like that dream catcher. Grandpa scoops me into his arms the way he used to when I was six. Usually I would mind, but not today. I relax when I feel that his arms are strong. Good.

Mom starts flipping the radio stations when they get in the car. *God, not classical again.* She tells me she's got a headache, and opens the window. A snowy egret flies by, headed over the water. We are at the edge of the bay marsh, north of the airport. She and Grandpa are not talking, just staring out the window. Stunted pine trees grow out of the pebbly beach. It is so quiet. I can't take it. I start talking.

"Mom, you're gonna be surprised. . . . the apartment is clean." I don't tell her that I locked out Jeanette, the housekeeper, and spent the day with my music blaring, scrubbing the entire place until my mind was clear.

The smell of salt and seaweed are blowing through the open window now. I breathe deeply and look in the rear view mirror. Grandpa has his eyes closed, but he's saying something.

"Stop the car, Annie. I want to get out."

Is he gonna get sick, maybe even throw up? AIDS can do that, I found from my reading. I stop the car south of Candlestick Park, San Francisco's windswept and almost always freezing park, on the upper edge of the salt marsh. Grandpa opens the car door and walks over to the edge of the water, where he squats down at its edge. He unlaces his hiking boots, pulls his shoes and socks off, and sticks his feet in the shallow waves. Birds are flying all around his head. They must be protected here—some sort of preserve. Even though we're only a few hundred feet away from the highway and the cars are loudly speeding past us, I hear him start to chant. Mom is frozen in the car and doesn't move or say anything. *Just what is going on now?*

"Mom, are you just gonna let him stay out there with his feet in the water? He could get sick!" I realize how crazy that sounds right after I've said it. He *is* sick. She doesn't say anything back; she's just staring at him. *What is wrong with her?*

I try again. "Somebody should be out there with him. You should go."

"Annie, he'll be okay. He's just saying his prayers."

"Someone needs to be with him." I get out and slam the car door. She makes me so angry. As soon as I'm outside the car, however, I want to get back in. *What am I going to say? I can't talk about it.*

I hear his voice singing, some kind of prayer—he has a soft, quivering baritone that breaks when he hits the high notes. Not only do we look alike, but we sound alike, too. I listen. . . . I can pick out some of his French, thanks to Mom for all those lessons.

But I feel it more than hear it. . . . other sounds that fall and rise with the afternoon wind. He gets up, holding his hands to the sky and looks at Mount Diablo poking through the clouds across the San Francisco Bay. I step up and stand beside him, looking at the small gray waves lapping at my boots. I feel so upset . . . but then I see. *I don't have to say anything. I am here with him.*

Modern Medicine

*M*y brother Marc, Dad, and I sit with the AIDS specialist in San Francisco, listening to him talk about living with HIV. I ask the question: "How did this happen?"

Marc moans. "Do you always have to act like a doctor? Look, it doesn't matter now." I don't say it—now is the worst possible time for a sibling quarrel. But, it does matter to me. If we know more maybe we can figure something out.

The specialist mumbles, "Patient confidentiality is important. Your father has rights, Doctor."

What does this guy think I want to know? I just want to help. He doesn't realize how important family is. Doctors don't live with their patients. And this is AIDS. We need to know. Dad looks at the specialist. "As the patient, I would respectfully like to know the percentage of infected blood in those heart machines that were used for my valve repair." Once he says it, I remember that Dad had a weak heart after having rheumatic fever in the orphanage.

The specialist stares at all of us not saying anything. Dad speaks again, "The valve repair six years ago—that machine took a lot of blood." The room is very quiet. Dad asks again, "What was the estimate of infected blood in those machines?"

The specialist speaks slowly. "Fifty percent of that blood was infected."

Fifty percent. "Then there are others who were infected."

"Yes, there are." I can't stop thinking—fifty percent infected—but Dad is moving on.

Three bottles of medicine are stacked on the physician's desk. Dad unscrews a bottle and shows us a silver pill the size of a walnut. . . . "only" three pills per day.

"A lot of horses must get this virus." Dad winks, and the doctor smiles.

Marc grunts. He is tired and irritated after his long flight from Montreal, and he wants us to be serious. "Look, Dad, you've got to attack this thing. You're the one who showed me how to do it—remember the big limestone rock in the tomato patch? I was gonna give up and plant around it, maybe even move the garden, but you kept me going. We built a pulley and worked for hours, leveraging the boulder out of there. You've gotta fight harder here." With this, Marc's voice breaks, his hand hits the desk, and the horse pills jump, some of them spilling out onto the floor. Lying on the carpet, they look even bigger than walnuts.

"Only three per day? I don't see any problem with that." Dad jokes, and this time we all laugh, even the doctor, until tears run down our cheeks.

On our way out of the doctor's office, we visit the pharmacy and pick up many more than three bottles. After paying for the precious silver walnuts, Dad and Marc decide that they want to have spaghetti with meatballs for lunch. We find a one-counter restaurant in North Beach. California vegetarian, I break my usual fast and join them, biting into large ground meatballs stuffed with onions and chopped parsley. Marc orders the wine, a dark bottle of sangiovese, and we drink, feeling its effects after only a glass.

Marc's sense of humor is back. He and Dad start laughing about where they can find a horse in San Francisco to test the pills on.

"Let's get the old roan that bucked you into the ocean, Elisabeth."

"No. . . . remember?" said Dad. "She held on—hours of bucking in the Pacific Ocean—and he couldn't get her off. It was the horse that finally gave up in exhaustion. We need tougher horses for these pills."

—Elisabeth

I am back at the bay marsh where Grandpa is wading, tracking a spotted seagull with my camera. Really, I am just pretending to be on a shoot, so that I don't have to go home. First, Grandpa comes to visit— now, Uncle Marc. And the apartment was crowded with just Mom and me. Men take up more room. They're taller, bigger . . . even their voices occupy more space. Why is that? I'm an alto, my voice is deep too, but drop it several notes further—guy-style—and the words seem to hang in the air. Grandpa's voice really holds on. "Good morning," is around for minutes.

Not that anyone is saying "Good morning" in the apartment now. Things are sort of tense, like they are all trying to be stoic—so they don't talk. And I think that this is something you gotta talk about. Mom says that they are talking. It's just not the kind of talking that she and I do. It's the quiet kind, despite their loud voices. I'm listening hard so I don't miss it, whenever it's gonna happen. But I'm gone a lot, like today— skipping school, taking my camera, pretending to shoot pictures. Out here I don't have to fake my feelings. A night gull swoops in front of Mount Diablo, and I snap it for Grandpa. He tells me that he likes Diablo the best of our mountains. There aren't exactly a lot to choose from. Mount Sutro is ruined by a giant spiky radio tower. White and red metal and flashing lights aren't what you want to see when you look at a mountain. Davidson has a concrete six-foot cross, so forget that one. Now, Tamalpais in Marin County, which is shrouded in fog, is my personal favorite. I like it a lot despite the fact that Grandpa made me climb it with him on my sixth birthday. Up close it is mostly steep gravel switchbacks. I tell him that I can appreciate it better from a distance.

It is on a Tamalpais switchback that I decide to tell Grandpa that I received a letter from my dad while Mom was in Chicago.

"Anaquad," he says. "How is he doing?"

"I don't care," I answer.

"Hmmm, I don't know, Annie."

"Don't know what?"

"Don't know that you don't care."

Grandpa is taking me on these hikes now so I can get ready for this road trip that he's planning—driving, camping, hiking. "You've got to be strong, Annie." He wants to leave soon and is trying to get Uncle Marc to go with us. I want Marc to go too, in place of me. They need someone to watch the apartment, take out the recycling, stay at home with warm running water and television. But Marc is refusing to go. He calls himself an air warrior, not a road warrior. I think that he's scared that Grandpa is gonna die on the trip. And he might be right. . . . I think Grandpa *wants* to die on the road. That's what it's really about—some sort of death ritual—and we've all got to be there. Now, Mom, I can understand. It's perfect for her. She gets off on saving people. She probably thinks she's gonna save him. Not me, I'm a realist like Grandpa. I know that medicine isn't gonna save him, and neither is Mom. He's going to die. I know it, and he knows it. The only question I've got is why do I have to be right there, watching it happen?

Grandpa is sitting alone in the living room when I get back from my photo shoot, and he's spread a whole stack of maps out on the floor. I want to go to my bedroom and muffle everything with loud music, not spend hours looking at maps, but I can't just leave him all by himself. I sit down with him, both of us cross-legged on the floor. I notice how flexible his body is and wonder when he will start to look sick.

"I want you to see this place, Annie—the wild part of the Wolf River, North of Shauno in Wisconsin. Your mom was fifteen the first time I took her there. We camped for five days just west of a waterfall that concealed a granite cave. Your mom loved that place. She would sit there for hours, just staring at the rocks . . ." His voice trails off and the room is silent. His fingertip is resting on the map, lodged between large patches of blue—the Great Lakes.

"Grandpa?" I ask. He's just staring at the map and doesn't answer me. "Grandpa!" This time I speak much louder.

"Annie . . ."

"Mom talked about it." I'm not sure I want to say more, to tell him what she had said. There was no mention of spacing out and staring at the cave.

"What did she say?"

"'People die,' she said. 'People die there.' She said that she had seen dead people there."

"Your mom said she saw the spirits?"

"No, I think she meant real people, Grandpa. She talked about watching this group of kids rafting from the University. Their raft snagged on a big rock, then got stuck in a whirlpool that sucked the raft through an underground passage. She said all the kids except one fell out of the raft before it disappeared."

Grandpa speaks now. "She would remember that. That college boy screamed louder than anything I'd ever heard, 'I can't see. . . . I can't see. . . .' He was a young college man. Big muscles and a small brain. He just kept wailing, 'Oh, god . . . it's so dark! I'm fucked!' Your mom and I were standing on the shore. We could tell that he was stuck behind the waterfall. I kept her from going in after him . . . had to hold myself back, too. Didn't tell her that I was thinking of going in or she would have thrown herself into that water first."

"Did that boy die, Grandpa?"

"Maybe. But he didn't die that day. Your mom and I joined our voice with the water and we began singing folk songs. I like to think that the boy heard us and decided to take his chances. Finally, he dove down, deep under the roaring waterfall and swam out. We met him downriver an hour later, drinking liquor with his buddies, telling a great story about how he had been saved by these spirits."

"You think he heard you?"

"I don't know if he did, Annie. I wouldn't bet on it. He just had to calm down enough to swim out."

"But no one died?"

"Not that day. Your mom was young then. When we got down river, she wanted to sit and have a beer with these giant kids with their polished muscles and their pea-brains."

"Did you stop her?"

"I wouldn't have stopped her from doing that." He was staring off now, stuck on something again. "She said people died there?"

"That's what she said."

"Maybe that's what she saw when she was staring at those rocks for so long. I had heard a story about the Wolf, but you hear things like that. Never saw them myself, though."

"Do you think one of those other college boys drowned, going over the falls?"

"No. They were too busy thinking about the beers they were gonna drink once they got downriver. They wouldn't listen to anyone. It was going to be their trip, their way. They let us know they were coming before we saw them, playing their transistor radio so loud. That is why they didn't hear the falls. Then they hit the rock, and their raft tipped on end and hung there several minutes before it flipped 'em. Their radio was blaring and they were scrambling, hanging onto the raft that was gonna pop at any time—gonna turn into a huge, flat balloon. Then their radio died. It's probably still lying on the bottom of that cave. And their raft sank. But they got themselves out. We couldn't have saved 'em."

"But you tried to help?"

"Yeah, we watched the whole thing while we sang for their spirits. Then after our beers, we drove all night to Red River."

Red River again. Sacred. Yeah, every family has its place where magical things happen. The Wolf doesn't compare to that place. For Grandpa, that's it. I don't want to get him started—not on that. I have an excuse. I need to develop these negatives at the school photo lab by dinner if I want to show them to Marc, who is threatening to leave. I like Grandpa's stories a lot, but I know that he's just getting going tonight and it's hard to stop him. Oh God, he's starting on his uncle, Red Otter. I know he believes that he's gotta tell me these things, especially now. But it's right now that I just can't listen. Does it mean he's dying? That story about the spirits—God, Grandpa has always been a realist. Is that why I can't listen?

When I tell him where I'm going, he offers to come with me to my high school. A grandfather wandering around high school—is it gonna be like this the whole time he's here? Doesn't he know that kids want—no, *need*—to be with their friends? It's not that I'm not proud of him or anything like that. I know that he's a cool guy for a grandfather... he actually likes to go to the Haight and he notices things that I don't, like the day he saw the park being fenced to prevent homeless people from sitting in it. Maybe I should just say yes. But then I imagine myself walking down Haight Street (I always take Haight)... what would it look like? Me and some old guy. That's what other kids would think. I tell him I'll be back in an hour, but it's more like two hours later that I finally walk out of the photo lab. I dodge people as I move back up Haight Street, staring at the shop windows ... multi-purpose pipes, secondhand books, fake turquoise.

I'm not late for dinner because dinner's later than usual—lucky for me since I stopped at the Haight Street free clinic to get tested for HIV. I'm technically a virgin but if Grandpa got it I can't be too sure. Climbing the stairs, I can smell the navy beans—Grandpa's the chef again. Beans and ham ... beans and beer ... just beans. Road food, Grandpa calls it. When I push open the front door and see maps over every inch of the living room floor, I realize that I am going to have a hard time getting out of this trip. Grandpa looks like he is sitting where I left him. Only the Wisconsin map with its Wolf River Rapids is gone, replaced by his old faithful, the heartland of Canada—Manitoba, so torn and taped that you have to draw lines in your mind to connect the roads that either don't line-up or connect to mystery places. It doesn't matter. He doesn't need a map to get there. The route is laid out in his mind. Uncle Marc is holding a new map, the California Coast. It spills out of a shiny turquoise-colored plastic folder, reminding me of the aquamarine ocean that Marc is detailing: the rock formations of Big Sur, the briny tide pools where we camped in third grade (not a place to go back to), the barking seals at Pescadero, and those fat, juicy oysters at Tamales Bay. It can be done by day trips, which means no crowded backseat or sleeping bags unraveled on hard-packed earth, no unknown animals night-howling and me awake. No one dies on that kind of road trip. At least, not me. But Grandpa is not ready for it.

"Marc, it's not what I'm thinking about. Sounds like you might even be planning to drive me to some kind of spa."

"Dad . . . you at a spa? I'd have to be crazy."

"But you were thinking it, so don't deny it. Mud baths, tarot card readings, customized sweat lodges. . . ."

"I need that . . . a spa vacation in Northern California." Marc smiles. "Just kidding, Dad."

But he's not. And he's right, too. We all need Marc's vacation. But there aren't gonna be any spas on our trip. Ours has to be on hard ground in isolated places. And it isn't supposed to be fun.

Dinner isn't fun either, though the beans are better than usual. "Olive oil is the secret, my girl." Grandpa lifts his eyebrows at me. I don't tell him that I can taste the beer in it, too. He needs to have some secrets. On a road trip, everyone is too close together. No secrets. They even know when you want to go to the bathroom.

Grandpa and Marc fight it out at the table while we eat. Maybe I just imagined the beer. The taste has kinda gone away as I've been eating it. Maybe it's 'cause beans are a strong food. Bland, but they overpower anything. I eat two big bowls so that I don't have to talk. California spa versus Red River saga. Mom's quiet, too, but finally I hear her voice. She's got some work thing—she's gotta go North to see this Hoopa girl who's been arrested. The girl is sixteen and they want to put her in jail for ten years, so they want a shrink for teens to see her.

"Why, Mom?"

"Her stepfather tried to touch her and she hit him with a metal lamp. Unfortunately, she hit him so hard that she broke his neck. She killed him."

"Ten years. . . . and she's my age! Don't they care?"

"They care that she's Indian."

"That helps her?"

"Like a black mark, Annie." I feel something right below the surface with her, but she's so careful, so controlled—perfect for a kid shrink—she's not gonna blow. How does she do it? More to the point, why does she do it?

Grandpa and Marc have stopped arguing and are listening to us now.

Marc speaks first, "Another saving, Sis. Do the judges listen to you now that you're older?" A scar on his upper lip twists into a jagged line, and I realize that Marc's angry even though his voice is slippery smooth.

"Somebody's got to do it, Marc." Mom's voice is really tired now. I know that he's trying to keep her from getting even more exhausted, but does he have to get so angry about it?

"So it's always gotta be you? How many reports have you written to save Indian kids? Do they ever listen? Oh, excuse me . . . those judges have to pay attention now because you're a doctor, don't they. How often have they done anything you said?"

Everyone is quiet. Until I speak.

"Mom, what does Marc mean?" I ask supportively, even though I've heard her talk about it before. She needs to hear herself say it. Mom is always saying how education makes a difference, gives you a voice, but I feel her giving up tonight. What's going on? Her undying optimism, is it going? Something has got her.

"Just what he says, Annie. He means that they—the judges, courts, juries—don't listen to arguments that explain why there are twice as many Indian kids in jail as white. And he's right. They don't listen. That's all." Mom stands up to make tea, something I know she does when she feels anxious. But this time she just stands there, holding the kettle and doesn't put it on the stove. She's trying to say something, doesn't want to blow up. Finally she says, "Look, Marc, I'm fed up with the whole thing too, but there has to be resistance to locking them up."

Grandpa looks over at Marc, then at Mom, and speaks very slowly.

"Elisabeth, where are you going this time?"

"North, almost the border. The lawyers from the tribal council said it was near Weitchpec."

"How far is it from Medicine Lake?"

"I don't know, Dad. Where's that?"

"North of the Pit River. East of Shasta. Not far from the Oregon border."

"You're thinking about going there, Dad? It isn't Red River . . . but I'd be willing to drive . . . or we could split it." Mom's voice has more energy.

"Me, too. But your dream, Dad. Red River. That we'd all go together," Marc speaks.

"Well, it's part of my dream. Angeline's spirit is in Red River. And they built this fancy grave for Riel that I wanted you kids to see. I want to see it. But my dream is to share my spirit with you. . . . all of you." And he looks at me.

Medicine Lake. It is decided.

Angeline – 1868

Among the Cree, the powers of ancestors are the driving force. Every newborn child is carefully examined for physical signs, such as a mole or birthmark, that might demonstrate a link with a particular deceased relative. If such a sign is found, the child will be given that person's name. This custom crosses gender barriers; thus, a girl baby bearing a mark associated with a man will be given a male name, and her character will be deemed influenced by him.

—Commentary on the Cree People by Norman Bancroft-Hunt,
North American Indians (Courage Books: 1992)

Red River

Ni maw maw (my mother) is named Strong Wind for the tough Chinook song that blows across southern Alberta during the frozen moons and can melt several feet of snow in less than an hour. I am named Bird With First Snow because I arrive in the month of *pawacakinasis-pism,* the frost exploding moon, during the blizzard of 1855. This reminds the elders of the great storm of 1825, a year when our largest herd of buffalo was trapped in a white cloud and froze to death while standing. *Ma tawnt* (my aunt) Red Crow, and *Nookoum* (my grandmother) are present at my birth and sing my birth song as the moon rises. That night the cabin is so cold that my birth blood freezes in scarlet patches on the mud floor. Shivering and exhausted, my mother cries out that she and her baby are going to die. Lacking enough blankets to warm them, my grandmother covers my body with her own and insists that my aunt cover my mother. In the morning, painted with my mother's blood, my aunt, Red Crow, is found dead, but Strong Wind, *Nookoum*, and I are alive.

On the day of my birth, my father drives a charette filled with beaver and buffalo skins across the heart of America from Winnipeg to Minnesota. He discovers that he has a daughter only three months later, when he returns home after the snow has melted. My mother is a full-blooded Cree Indian who speaks many languages, among them French, Cree, and the mixed patois of their union—Prairie Tongue. My father, Jean Kirouac, is part Assiniboine, part French. He calls himself Métis, part of a hybrid culture of Assiniboine, Sioux, Cree, Scots, and French, a nation of mixed bloods. We live near Lake Winnipeg, a remnant of the ancient Lake Agassiz, in a fertile farmland where the Assiniboine and Red rivers join in a land called Assiniboia.

My father is a *coureur de bois*, a trapper of beaver and muskrat who, assisted by my mother, sets his snares in the cottonwoods and willows that line the Red and Assiniboine Rivers. For several months of the year he follows this course alone, sleeping outside on the furs that he hunts and trades. When I am young, the small animals that he traps leave our land, running north to the golden aspen, reaching the pine and fir forests that line the frozen sea. They escape after they learn the tricks of the crafted rawhide and wood neck-snapping seeds that my father and the others planted. After they disappear, my father worries about how he will care for my brothers and me. Hungry, he and the other trappers join together to chase the great animal that shares its life with my mother's people . . . the buffalo. Using guns and horses, they travel in packs of thousands seeking out their prey and returning to my home laden with heavy burdens, the remains of the carcasses of the huge animals on homemade carts that groan and creak from the weight of the dead. After they arrive, we feast for weeks, puffing out our bellies until we can eat no more, lying on the ground unable to move.

It is then that the whiskey traders from Hudson Bay visit and freely give my people brown water, seducing them with its hidden magic and dreams that promise great power. With whiskey comes fighting. I learn that a drinking man can kill his enemies and, as he drinks more, kill his friends. After one "gift" from the traders, my older brother, He Who Moves With the West Wind, knifes my younger brother, Red Otter, as he sucks out the last drops of a bottle. Blood spurts from little brother's neck until *ni maw maw* presses a piece of bark over it. My mother is learning about blood and bone medicine from our tribe's healer. I move close to her and watch. Very slowly, the blood flow ceases, and Red Otter smiles. My mother is not smiling. She looks at my father and speaks, "You brought this poison into our home and now it has infected our sons. It cannot stay here." She kicks the empty bottle on the floor and it rolls, stopping only after it hits my father's foot. He does not look at my mother, but picks up the bottle and nods. My older brother jumps up, spits into the air between our parents and jerks the bottle from our father's hand. My mother raises her hand and reaches for the bottle. He Who Moves With the West Wind steps toward my mother, his muscles tense and eyes burning, but she stops him with only one word, "Leave." He struts out of our cabin, but I hear the bottle crash and break when he staggers and falls on the large rocks outside the door. Red Otter stands up, holding his wound, and stumbles outside to find his brother. My mother and father do not speak. We sit and wait until my two brothers return, Red Otter now cradled in our older brother's arms. That night, *Nookoum* and Strong Wind tell my older brother that he cannot live there if he continues to accept the trader's gifts. The next morning my older brother leaves our home.

While watching my brother push his few possessions into a bundle, I question my mother's words for the first time. "*Ni maw maw*, why must He Who Moves With the West Wind leave home?"

She does not answer me, but begins cutting the winter squash into pieces and hands me a knife to cut with her. Later that night, she tries to talk with me about the fire poison. "Bird with First Snow, I love your brother but he is unable to refuse the brown water. It is poisoning his body and if he stays it will spread to you, your younger brother, your children, our family."

Looking into her eyes, I plead with her to let my brother stay—"I will not be poisoned by the brown water. I am strong."

"You are strong, but brown water does not respect the strength of our people."

In the days after my brother leaves, I spend time alone and shrug off *Nookoum*'s soft touches and my mother's attempts to make me talk. I even refuse to eat her meadow blueberries and softened pemmican. I understand that she is missing my brother as much as I am, probably more. He is her oldest son and, during the moons before he left, I observed them lying in the prairie grass watching the night spirits and talking together long after everyone was asleep. I agree with her decision that he cannot remain in our house if he is drinking liquor. I also see that he is strangely vulnerable—often falling on the floor, babbling, after only a few sips. And he cannot stop there, often drinking until he finishes the bottle and wets himself. I see that Red Otter watches him too closely. I understand why my mother asked him to leave, and I agree with her. But still I am angry with her. That is what I don't understand.

After my brother leaves, my father stops drinking. He spends more time at home and teaches Red Otter and me how to ride. I am skillful on a horse, and he gives his word that I can ride alongside him in the great buffalo chase. He promises me that I, a girl, will ride with the men. Twice a year, my people track and kill the buffalo on the plains. With the beaver and other animals gone, it is the only way we can live. To us, these hunts are both a time of celebration and a time of backbreaking work. For more than half a moon we ride, slaughter, and sleep.

During the year I become a woman, the carts gather early in *sagipukawipizum*, the moon that rises when the leaves come out, for the trip to Pembina, the site of the great hunts. Thousands are going. *Nookoum* and her sisters are driving five carts. My mother stays home to farm, but many of the women and all of the men prepare to go. I practice riding with my father, pretending that we are chasing buffalo cows. Running the herd, he calls it. We ride side by side, imagining a cow between us, pushing close together so that my father can aim and fire. He teaches me how to use a gun in case I have to shoot. "They don't always run the direction you want them to, Ange." The night before we leave, a group of the men come to our house to speak with my father. They point at me. "She can go but she can't ride with us. Put her in the wagon with the others." They nod at the women in my family who are silent, packing things for our journey. My father shouts the French words that he will not teach me, then follows them with "She rides with me, not with you." He rises, his fist raised, and moves towards their leader. *Nookoum* steps in between the men and my father. "She rides with him, or we don't skin your buffalo and they rot in the field." The hunters know that they need the women for the harvest. Without us, they cannot prepare the hides or preserve the meat. The men leave our home.

The next day I ride out of Red River beside my father. *Nookoum* follows, leading her sisters and our ox carts. Five days later, after joining thousands of my mother's people, the prairie Cree and other Métis, we meet the great buffalo. At a distance, they look like dark spots, some alone, others in groups. Closer, I can see that they are always moving—chewing and swallowing grass, steadily waving their tails in the wind.

We are there just before the mating fights begin. My first day with the buffalo is a long one. My father and the other men lift their guns and shoot across the prairie aiming for the largest bulls first, raising clouds of dust from the bronze grass into the air. Soon I can't see or breathe. Things are moving fast. We are riding in pairs now, encircled by the storm of pounding hooves. My father shouts orders, "*Droite*," and, "*Plus vite.*" I ride my horse quickly, driving full-grown animals toward him. His gun is firing, creating even more smoke, dust, and thunder, but we are successful. That day, we kill many buffalo. After the guns stop, I see that bleating calves are separated from their dead mothers; I hear the living mothers snort and call out for their missing children, and I know that they are a family like mine.

That night *Nookoum* teaches me the prayer of gratitude to the animals who share their lives with us, giving us food, shelter, and clothing. She prays while she skins the animals that are still lying where they fell on the ground. I talk to her about my feelings for the buffalo, and she tells me that she feels that way, too. We cut the meat into long strips and later hang them over a fire to smoke. She teaches me how to rub a sharp oval stone against the hides, cleaning the fat off the inside. The skin is hot against my hand, still warm from the buffalo's blood. Flecks of soft yellow fat and red flesh harden under my fingernails, painfully swelling them, but we do not stop, moving from one animal to the next, stripping four buffalo that evening. Fires dot the prairie that night as pairs of women climb over the carcasses, working together to butcher the animals before their bodies become too cold and stiff. My lessons continue until sunrise as *Nookoum* talks and sings, instructing me on how we will use their bones for scrapers, stomachs for *médecines*, and bull's organs for rattles. She tells me that even the calves' hides are used to swaddle our babies. Then she lets me sleep for two hours before I ride again with the men. That day, I ride as if in a dream. I no longer see the mothers and calves or hear their cries when they are separated. Little Buffalo Runner works tirelessly, driving the cows toward my father and the other hunters, jerking me awake when my body begins sliding into sleep. That night, I do not join the women's fires and instead sleep on the hard ground next to my father. Ten days we hunt and ten nights the women work. Exhausted, we leave the plains. I ride home on top of the hides that we scraped and will later tan with *Nookoum* and her sisters. I thank *Nookoum* for standing up for me with the Métis men so that I could ride in the hunt. She laughs. "Remember, Little Bird, let them know that you have something that they want. You have to be able to trade."

Three days west from Red River the air begins to stink. As we ride further we see why. Lying in the moving sea of grass are thousands of buffalo, rotting, stripped only of their skins and tongues—a delicacy stolen, my father says, for people who never even knew our land. Thousands of animals shot only for their tongues alone. The shrieks of the calves and the dying pierce the air. We have entered a living burial ground. I cover my face with my mother's fine embroidered linen cloth and urge my oxen to drive harder to escape the stench and the suffering. Against my father's wishes, my grandmother stops all of our carts. Looking at my father and pointing at the suffering animals, she says, "Kill them." My father obeys. Then *Nookoum* and her sisters prepare the ritual for the dead. They draw a circular design in the grass with a burning stick. Then they stand holding hands in the center. I remember that Grandmother invited me to join her during the days of the hunt when she honored the buffalo that we killed. Until sunset my grandmother and aunts stand chanting, thanking the generous buffalo for giving their lives to the missing hunters. Finally, after the roar of my father's gun ended, *Nookoum* lies in the sea of grass and digs her fingers into the earth. I kneel by her, watching.

That night, unable to sleep, I ask *Nookoum*, who is lying next to me, why she dug her fingers into the earth. She whispers, "The buffalo are holy; so is hunting. When I touch the earth, I find the animals and thank them. They give themselves to us. It is a great gift. We take only what we need. This is not what you have seen today—hunters who kill them for their tongues, and then leave them to rot. Soon, the buffalo will no longer come to us." Her eyes look dark and sad as she unbraids and strokes my hair. "Little Bird, we are the buffalo."

Buffalo Dream

*O*vercome with exhaustion, I wrap up in a soft blanket next to *Nookoum*'s warm body and listen to the whistling music of blowing grass. The west wind, *shawanung-nizeo*, a generous fellow, kind to hunters, is singing. Calmed, I fall into a deep sleep and have a strange and wonderful dream. In it, I lie down on the prairie next to the buffalo. I am stripped naked, rubbed with buffalo oil. My skin is painted the deep brown of their hides. In my dream the buffalo have their skins restored. Slowly, noiselessly, they arise from the earth and begin to dance with the pulsing music of the night. I lie in the cool grass unable to move, watching the graceful animals weave through the air above me. I begin to feel a strange tingling between my legs and my nipples grow hard and pointed. The oil on my body warms, heated by nothing that I can see. Then, one large buffalo separates himself from the others and moves overhead, lying close above my body. Unlike his brothers, this buffalo is a pale yellow, a rare shade that my father and the other hunters have talked about but never seen. The buffalo's horns are curved, long, and reflect the sky's light. He pushes them down to the earth on each side of me, so close I cannot see him clearly. But I feel the rising moon in his dark eyes, sucking me in. He, too, is covered with animal oil and slowly begins to rub his heavy body against mine, while he swings his head up and down marking his territory on both sides of my head. The feeling between my legs grows stronger and my calves begin to dance, moving in rhythm with the golden buffalo. We dance together, stronger and stronger, I raise my hips off the ground, until I finally feel my body join with his. We enter each other, slowly, painlessly, then pull back. At that moment, I feel my power. The rest of this dream I do not remember. I wake up with my arm wrapped around *Nookoum*, her breath on my neck, and discover that we are near home, moving along the west fork of Red River.

Once we return to Red River, my mother is back in charge. Overseeing the cooking for the week of feasting, she supervises the drying of the buffalo meat into the chewy muscles, pemmican, showing me how to sweeten its sharp, salty flavor with cranberries and other dried winter fruits. My brother and I have to help her, along with the aunts and a band of friends and neighbors, spending our days sunk to the earth, scraping vegetables, lifting racks of pemmican and stirring buffalo broths and stews. We work all day, but she insists we rest in the late afternoon and play games with the other children. I want to ride my horse, now honored with the name Little Buffalo Runner, at the annual jig, our celebration dance. As the sun sets, my father teaches me how to make "Little Buffalo" dance to the music just as we practiced riding the herd.

"Little Buffalo Runner is your spirit sister, Ange. Pay attention! You and she have to listen and dance as one." Papa's face turns red and he yells often, as I have a hard time moving my horse to the beat, let alone picking up the complicated rhythms that he is hoping I can manage. Finally, he invites the gifted fiddlers of the region to our home, hoping that their enticing beats will inspire my dancing with my horse. He is still disappointed in me, although it is fortunate that Little Buffalo keeps a steady tempo, even when I cannot guide her. I am bothered by my father's sudden anger. Ten days at the hunt and not a harsh word. But I know my father is a proud man and that he is looking forward to dancing with our horses together at the upcoming feast. Father and daughter herded the buffalo together, but in the fury of the hunt and hidden by dust clouds and stampeding animals, no one saw that. The jig will be different; everyone will be there and people will notice.

Strong Wind worries that my father's plan will bring some trouble and mentions the men's visit on the night of the hunt, but she, too, is proud of how well I rode. She and *Nookoum* take it upon themselves to teach me rhythm and sway with sensuous snake-like movements learned from their ancestors as they lift and rotate the racks of drying buffalo (hoping that they will impart some of their magic to me). They sew the costume that I will wear, matched with the other fifty riders—blue wool, brass buttons, leather moccasins, and the red, yellow and black woven silk sash of the Métis.

I await the night of the dance with the same great fear that I felt before the hunt and beg my horse for help. "Spirit Sister, help me dance with the others," praying for dance, a betrayal of the prayers that *Nookoum* taught me. The evening finally arrives, and I take my place next to my father on the prairie stage and move in rhythm with the fifty other riders on horseback. Little Buffalo Runner does not let me down and follows the other horses in the march, bowing and pirouetting. I feel the rhythm in her body and she and I move as one. I catch my father's eye at the end of the fastest steps and see that he is smiling. His daughter can hunt and dance.

After the grand square dance is performed on horseback, I search out *Nookoum*'s and Strong Wind's faces and see that my dancing has brought honor to my family. I do not see the small angry group of men who again confront my father, this time condemning him for permitting his daughter to dance on horseback. "These are military maneuvers for men," they shout. I do see a drunken overweight man with a small sharp knife cut the sleeve of my father's flannel jacket—the one that my mother spent hours making for the ceremonial jig. Blood soaks through the new wool and my father holds his arm tightly trying to push it back in. Then a man with dark shadowed eyes and a full beard steps forward. I later hear that only this man spoke in favor of my dancing with the men, and his name is Louis Riel. Helping my mother bandage my father's cut, I ask my parents about him. My father tells me that Louis is a French-speaker, a Catholic who studied to be a priest in Montreal. He mentions that this man has visions for our people. Thinking of how he stood up for my dancing, I ask whether his visions include women. My father does not know. I remember the name of this man. I am learning that most men are not like my father. Most men do not want their daughters to ride with the buffalo.

Months later, my father takes me to hear Riel in the church in Saint Boniface. There, I learn that Riel is the son of a man who had also been a leader among our people. People call Riel *"Le Jeune,"* but he does not look young to me. However, it is difficult to say exactly how he appears to me, because of the strange warmth I feel whenever I try to meet his gaze. I look away, but even hearing his voice gives me some of those same feelings—heat, and the sense that I am flying, a wild bird moving in the rafters. Overwhelmed by these sensations, I can still hear him perfectly. Riel's clear voice touches those rafters and speaks of freedom for oppressed peoples who live under the rule of others. He does not want us to become one of those people. His tone softens when he describes my mother's people and mentions that they, too, have rights and will be part of this future. He describes our people as a joining together of many into one, and says that it gives us strength. I am deeply moved, and sit in the church long after my father and the other men leave. My father asks me to go with him, worried that I will be hurt, never forgetting the man who stabbed him, but when I tell him I want to stay he lets me. Sitting alone, I understand that if Riel has to strongly argue for the basic rights of my mothers' people, then there must be those who believe that they do not have those rights. Growing up in Red River, where Indians, Métis, Scots, French, and others live together, I hadn't thought that it might be different in other places, or that others might see us differently. I share Riel's view of the strength in our mixed blood, and I know that his visions are important. I am surprised that he can reveal a vision so powerful in a Catholic Church. My mother and *Nookoum* tell me that the Catholic Church smothers visions. *"Don't dream there, Little Bird, because the spirits will be unable to find you and you will lose your faith."* Listening to Louis, I realize that the Catholic Church allows some people to find their dreams.

Like Louis, my mother's people have strong visions, too. Unlike my older brother, I will not be sent out alone to the prairie to fast and wait for the spirits. Starving, thirsting manboys run across the sweet grass or climb the sacred rocks, until, exhausted, they fall asleep and are visited by the great spirits. During his spirit time, when my older brother finally sleeps on the smooth grey lake stones that hold Lake Winnipeg, a river otter appears to him, carrying dried buffalo meat softened with summer plums, holding a leather skein of cool water. Refreshed, my brother wakes and returns to our people.

A crowd of awed younger boys gather around him, many reaching out to touch him, hoping to share the powerful magic that he has just experienced. *Nookoum* asks him if the otter spoke to him. "No," he answers, "it just smiled and brought me food and drink." I see my parents standing quietly on the outskirts of the crowd that has gathered around my brother. I notice that their fingers are touching. They do not speak directly to my brother but smile proudly, blessing his victory. Remembering my night on the prairie with the golden, dancing buffalo, I want to talk with my brother about his vision—touching, smelling, feeling things—but I do not.

Girls are not sent out to search for spirits, but it is believed instead that the spirits come to us, comforting and stilling our terrors during the time of our monthly blood. I question *Nookoum*, telling her that I am neither afraid, nor visited by spirits when I bleed. She listens and does not ask me any questions. I do not tell her about my buffalo dream.

Métis Nation

My last year in Red River, 1869, is marked by constant fighting. A newly forming "Canadienne" government in Toronto is struggling for control of our land. My father says that the fur trading companies believe that they own us and can sell us to anyone they want to. Fearing that this will happen, my father and the other Métis join with my mother's people to make a provisional government where all will be seen equally—"all" being "all men"—whether Indian, Métis, or white. Disappointed, I wonder if others notice that women are not mentioned. Louis Riel is elected president of our government—a cause for celebration. Words blow across the plains to the east and then back to Red River that our ideas are causing much trouble in Toronto. We are called a government of illiterate Indians and half-breeds who will be unable to rule ourselves. We are also told that our existence interferes with the prosperity of Canada. My father and the others compose a different story. We want to rule ourselves, and if this is not possible, then at least we wish to choose who will rule us. Our lives are changing; the small animals that we trapped are now all gone and my father says the buffalo are leaving too. When he tells me this, I am afraid, remembering *Nookoum*'s words, "We are the buffalo." My father is worried that others will come and steal the rich farmland that my mother works. He is not the only one who speaks about these things. *Ni maw maw* and *Nookoum* argue in Cree with their relatives who come to visit. They tell stories about others who fought for their lands. I listen. "If we are to survive, we must resist," *Nookoum* says. "And we may still die."

Our government in Saint Boniface exists for almost a year before hundreds of red-coated men travel from Toronto, transported across the great inner sea, Lake Superior, riding north to Red River. Now, herds of soldiers patrol the streets of Saint Boniface and Red River searching for the leaders of the Provisional government. My father and the other leaders hide in makeshift huts on the edge of the river, sneaking into barns to warm themselves with the cows and horses. We are called rebels, and our leaders, traitors, by the men in Toronto. Our free government ends. My father explains that whether we are freedom fighters or rebels depends upon perspective. The men in Toronto have the perspective of distance—they do not live in these lands—and power—these men in Toronto also have soldiers and money.

One night, a crowd of soldiers comes to our home, jeering and shouting, "Drunken half-breeds and Indians, give us your leaders." They speak to my father, asking him where Louis Riel is. When my father refuses to answer them, they throw rocks at his legs until he falls, then hit his head with their rifle butts, splitting the skin on his scalp. Finally, they gag and drag him out of our house. I try to run after them, but *Nookoum* sees the soldiers staring at me and holds me back. Held by her, I cannot speak. What I see is so horrifying, I have no memories of my feelings. I remember working, *Nookoum* and my mother giving me small tasks— tending fire, feeding animals—to keep me moving, to forget the image of my father's bleeding skull.

A week later I discover my father dumped in my mother's potato garden, still alive but shaking with a night fever that he caught in prison. I feel the raised pus-filled spots on his face explode on my fingers, and after I unbutton his shirt, I see that they are spreading slowly to his chest. After a moon passes, he stops breathing. *Nookoum* says that he died from the loss of his dream.

I join my mother, who is at my father's feet, staring at his legs, too frightened to look at his swollen, blistered head, and *Nookoum* who is singing the Cree death chant for my father—*Tawnshikiya*. Together, we wash his body and wrap him in a buffalo hide saved from my first hunt. Then we carefully carry him to his burial place at the edge of Red River, where we cover him with a mound of soft orange mud, pine needles, and river stones. That night, *Nookoum* and I ride north on Buffalo Runner and she points to the northern stars in the night sky. Together, we search for my father.

"Bird With First Snow, the *Choepi* ghosts, the spirits of our people who haunt the night sky, are having a good time, but he is not dancing with them yet. He will be there soon. I promise you." Again I believe and search the northern sky each night for my father's spirit which I know will rise high shining in the dark with the rest of my family who left our earth.

It is after we bury my father that they begin to talk about another future for me. I hear them singing—*"Little bird must leave, it's no longer safe here"*—but I don't listen at first. I don't want to leave them or my home. I am just beginning my life as a young woman. But when *Nookoum* says I have to find a way to escape, that others will soon die, I listen to her. She gives me her blessing and a bag that she embroidered with beadwork flowers and pine needles, saying softly, "For your children." This warms my heart because at this moment I believe that I will be the last one. She encourages me to go with the first group of Métis that will move to the Western Illinois French colonies on the Mississippi. She chooses the destination for my journey after listening to the stories of other Métis. She tells me, "Riel will go there" and the *Choepi*. "They too will follow you, your spirit will be safe, and you can save your children." *Nookoum* promises me that the *Choepi* will follow. And I believe her.

We travel hundreds of miles across the prairie, packed into charettes, flat-based wooden carts with two oversized wheels, the carts that we used to transport the buffalo hides through the northern sea and forests. While traveling to Illinois, I stare at the northern lights searching for my father's ghost. It is this hope alone that keeps me alive walking away from my family. I feel alone although many flee with me, and

Nookoum and Strong Wind promise to follow. I hug the bags of healing herbs that they have made for me, wishing I could hold them in my arms.

      I believe that it is my father's death, even more than the failed resistance, that caused the break-up of my family. If he lived, I know that Strong Wind would have stayed in Red River. Without him, my family was in danger when the Toronto soldiers moved in—my mother, as an Indian woman, is seen as less than human. Even at fifteen, I understand that being less than human is now my life, too.

In Exile

*T*he snow comes early during our first winter in exile, arriving in *Kastatinopizun*, the moon when the rivers begin to freeze. Our American relations are kind, openly sharing their homes with us, the displaced Métis. I stay at a farm with many others who have fled Red River. The Illinois women invite me to sit at their hearths and tell my story. I try. I visit their cabins, drink their healing teas, and listen to their tales, but I cannot open my mouth. One woman, Elisabeth Junot, speaks gently to me and when she sees that I cannot answer, she holds me. Although I am taller than she is, I sit in her lap and she rocks me, singing songs of her mother's people—the Ojibwa. Our songs are similar, Cree and Ojibwa sharing *Choepi* ghosts dancing in the night sky and French partners in bed. My voice wants to join her, but my heart will not let me.

When the snows deepen, Elisabeth straps *rachets* (snowshoes) to our feet and shows me her country. She shares the secrets of her winter *médecines*—swamp root, winter cattails. She is holding my arm when they bring news that Strong Wind and *Nookoum* have died in the northern sea trying to come to me, and that my younger brother, Red Otter, has disappeared. A fire seizes my stomach and I still cannot speak, but their songs are chanting in my head for days. During the nights, I search the sky for *Choepi*, looking and asking, *"Are you there yet? Any of you?"*

In my head I sing over and over again the songs we sang for the dead buffalo, echoing *Nookoum*'s words, "We are the buffalo, Little Bird, remember." Not only do I remember—my problem is that I cannot forget. Singing their songs and recalling their words reminds me that she and my mother are not with me. Repeating, "We are the buffalo . . ." over months I come to feel the words differently. No longer am I gripped by a pain in my stomach. Instead, I feel the power that I experienced when the yellow buffalo entered me in my dream. And I am finally able to sleep.

After many months pass, my voice returns to me. Not long after I begin to speak again, one of the other exiled people, a silver-haired farmer named Leon Beaucoeur, asks me to marry him. I refuse. I want my mother, my father, my people. To him these things do not matter. He wants me.

Many encourage me to consider his proposal. He is, after all, a Métis, and he too fled Red River. Others tell me that he has an interest in politics. It is a reasonable choice. But I do not think that way. I receive word from my brother, He Who Moves With the West Wind, who has escaped to Batouche, far west of Red River. He invites me to join him, telling me that many of my mother's people are there, and he writes that they will die with the buffalo. I remember the magic of the hunts and am tempted to follow him, but I choose not to after recalling his drinking and how it led him to leave our home. And, even more than that, I want to live with the buffalo, not die with them. Rumors reach our colony that the buffalo are being slaughtered. No longer able to share their lives with the buffalo, my mother's people are being herded into camps where many starve and die from disease. I think of returning to Red River where I know the land so well— trapping, farming, a life that would be familiar. But stories have reached us from Red River. The Métis are suffering. Their lands are being taken. Elisabeth encourages me to stay in the colony. She entices me with her magic healing herbs, showing me how to use them as medicine and promises that she will teach me to read and write in French. Like my father, I speak many languages, but unlike him, I have not made friends with the pen.

During the first winter, Louis Riel, our exiled leader, visits our colony. He now has a five thousand dollar price fixed on his head by

John MacDonald, Canada's leader. He spends much time with Leon and the other men discussing politics—how those who fled south can help the situation in Red River. I attend meetings with Elisabeth and the other Métisses, where Riel, who remembers my parents, recognizes me. He steps down from the pulpit of St. Anne's and walks straight toward me stopping to say, "You wore the uniform of the Métis and rode in the buffalo dance, daughter of Kirouac!" I sit frozen to the maple wood seats that we built in our reconstructed church, my head lowered; I know that I am blushing, the buffalo dance unfolding around us. "She likes to read, too," announces Elisabeth, who is sitting next to me. Elisabeth then tells him about my small collection of books and he volunteers to share his with me. At the time I am almost sixteen and he is twenty-seven.

Not long after this, Riel leaves to speak at another Métis colony after giving me several books. Elisabeth Junot speaks with Leon Beaucoeur and tells him that she believes that I am too young to marry. She offers me a refuge from Beaucoeur's entreaties, a small cabin near her own, and together Elisabeth and I collect wild medicines and share them with those who come to us. A history of American herbs that was published in Montreal is one of the books that Riel left with me when he left to visit other parts of America to seek money for the Métis cause. In it, I discover descriptions, sometimes even finely drawn sketches, of the plants that Elisabeth and I cut from the bottom of the swampy trees lining the Illinois rivers. I read it carefully, marking the herbs that we know and sharing my knowledge with my friend. She suggests that I correspond with Riel, who is traveling to other colonies. Beginning modestly, I send him a brief note describing our discovery that a finely ground paste of *la vosh di peup* (red pipestone) could be used to treat skin boils. When he responds with a lengthy letter congratulating us on our work, I answer him, and we begin a regular correspondence. He, too, has a strong interest in medicine and chronicles the herbs that he has seen in the other colonies that he has visited. Through him I discover uses for *l'arb du Saent Jean* and *bel angelique*. Although I hear from a Métis flatboat rider on the Mississippi that my younger brother, Red Otter, is receiving an "education" in an Ojibwa school, and that my older brother is still chasing the buffalo, the letters from Riel are the only ones that I receive. They increasingly bring me pleasure.

For several years I live quietly with Elisabeth, collecting and cataloguing the herbs of Illinois while I educate myself. I read the newspapers from Red River, searching for information about my family and Riel. Exiled from Canada, Louis Riel travels widely in the United States and its territories, pleading the cause of our people—the displaced Métis. When he is in the US, I receive regular communications from him in which he reviews and encourages my education. I also receive cosseted letters when he sneaks home to see his mother and his supporters who remain in Canada. Although he is exiled and a bounty was offered for his capture, he runs for the National Canadian Parliament and wins, taking office in 1874. For a brief period, he receives amnesty, but is then expelled from the House of Commons and again exiled from Canada for five years.

At this point, his letters to me change. Now, he begins each letter by calling me his *chère mère noire* and tells me that he and I, together, will found a great nation. I am unclear about what he means by this. He tells me that he is planning another visit to the United States soon to meet with President Grant and other Washington politicians in order to seek support for our people. He tells me he will visit me then.

During the month of the exploding sky, Elisabeth is away and Louis stays with me in my cabin. He brings news of my family. My oldest brother has joined the smooth-tongued Cree chief, Poundmaker, in the Far West in search of the dying buffalo. Louis also tells me that he saw my little brother in Red River, newly released from the Indian School. In addition to news, Louis brings treasured books and a desire to have a child with me—his *petite chère mère noire*. He believes that he is David, a prophet of the white French God, and that it is our path to have children together. He tells me that David suffered great hardships and, like our people, was forced to live in a foreign land. When he says, "our people," I realize that he sees me as one of them, a Métisse. This comment causes me to think differently about myself. Before this, I thought of my father as Métis and my mother as Cree, but saw myself only as a refugee living in a foreign land. Louis says that I am part of the dream that he has for the Métis people. I listen—my mother's people have always admired those with sacred dreams, believing that their visions tell the future. Even if I did not believe in dreams, I still would have laid down with Louis Riel.

We spend much of our first night talking in front of my cabin fire. I tell him stories of *Nookoum* and Strong Wind. He remembers my father's words. We share our education. He tells me about his religious and legal training in Montreal, and I show him my growing studies in herbs and medicine. Louis is a poet who murmurs magical words that start with *chère mère noire* and end on the plains of Canada. He brings the sharp clean smells of the prairie grass and the light of the night stars. I know that I am no longer alone.

We spread out on the buffalo hides that I have tanned. I feel the return of the pale yellow buffalo that I met on the prairie. This time the buffalo is not dancing with me, but watching me with Louis, guiding our way.

After the fire dies down, we become dream riders, mounting each other until, exhausted, we fall asleep at sunrise. And, although these nights will soon be gone forever, I remember them.

Louis leaves me just before the rise of *pawacakinasis-pism*, the frost exploding moon, and travels to Washington, DC, believing that he will meet with the President of the United States. He is filled with excitement, and word soon reaches our colony that he has met with President Grant. Then, nothing for several moons. I wonder what has happened—where is he?

One day, Leon Beaucoeur comes to speak with me. He is running for political office, hoping to represent the Métis colony in Springfield.

I notice that his eyes are blue, his hair silver. Louis has brown hair and eyes. Leon speaks to me carefully as if he has rehearsed what he is about to say. "Angeline, have you heard that our leader claimed to have seen a vision of his God in St. Patrick's Cathedral, the great church in Washington, DC? He said that the French God told him that he was a great prophet who would found a nation." It is strange to hear Leon speak about Louis and the visions that Louis has already confided in me. I sense that he is waiting to see my reaction and wonder why he is telling me this. Not yet understanding, I struggle to keep my face clear of feeling. Has something happened to Louis? Is this why he has neither visited nor communicated with me? When Leon does not speak further, I ask him if he knows what happened to Louis. He does not look at my face as he speaks. "They have locked him up in an asylum for crazy people, Angeline. It is where he belongs."

Our conversation ends not long after this. I can feel my fear and sadness pushing into my face, and I do not want Leon to see it. Elisabeth is still gone, and there is no one for me to share my feelings with.

Although the snows are high, I leave my cabin and hike through the drifts to the river, where I camp and fast. I do not eat until I discover that I am carrying Louis's child.

Ayikipism, The Frog Moon

*M*y son is born during the rise of *Ayikipism,* the frog moon. His welcoming cry joins hundreds of small voices living in the pond nearby my cabin. Louis does not return. He sends word with a Hudson Bay trader delivering pelts that our son should be named Joseph, and that he, too, will be a savior of our people.

I write to the hospital of Saint Jean de Dieu in Montreal, where Elisabeth finally discovers that Louis is being treated, inquiring about his condition, but do not receive a reply. I collect the flowers of arnica, a thistle used to treat brain shock, and the bark of red willow for brain fever and mail it to the hospital. I pray, not to the Catholic God that has captured Louis's mind in the Grand Cathedral in Washington, but to the God of my mother's people, asking, "Save Louis from his dreams." For a long time, I wonder how the God in Washington stole the missions of my Buffalo lover. Where have those dreams gone? Dreams of a world where all beings—buffalo, women, and men lived freely. I still believe the dream, but I know that Louis is gone. Elisabeth encourages me to continue to write him. It is her faith in me and my relationship with Louis that keeps me hopeful.

When Joseph can sit alone at the edge of the pond and play with the frogs, I hear that Louis has left the hospital and traveled to the Far West, still seeking to form a nation where my people, the Métis, and all immigrants will be equal. I also hear that he is living in the cabin of another Métisse. I no longer write to him. *Nookoum* and *ni maw maw* did not tell me who steals the dreams of lovers. I do not believe it is the

Catholic God. I wonder if Louis sacrificed his dream with me for dreams with others.

When my son, Joseph, has seen eight winters, his father is imprisoned and hanged for "treason" along with seven of my mother's people in 1885. The Métis dream for equality of people of all races is over. The Defense bases its principal argument on Riel's madness. He is found guilty and dies beginning his search for the *Choepi*.

It is during the longest day of that year that I allow Leon Beaucoeur into my life. I explain it to myself by saying that he knew my parents and the Métis dream, all of which are now dead. I ignore my own dreams, which keep telling me that Leon does not know me.

Gilles – 1924

May 6, 1885

*T*he Spirit of God made me realize the extent of the rights which the Indian possesses to the land of the North-West. Yes, the extent of the Indian rights, the importance of the Indian cause are far above all other interests. People say the native stands on the edge of a chasm. It is not he who stands on the edge of a chasm; his claims are not false. They are just.

—Louis Riel (Métis leader)

Red Otter

*D*amn, I didn't want to come to this place. A pull stop in the middle of a dead cornfield. Not even a real train station. I was gonna run. But they knew that, so the director has his assistant ride the train with me, a goon with iron arms that never let go of me. When we are leaving Chicago, I hear him say to the conductor, "I'm not supposed to take my hands off this dirty half-breed until I see the Indian woman." That's me he's talking about—the dirty half-breed. And that's not the worst name he calls me. When old Chunky Arms finally shoves me out the train door, I hear him mutter, "Bad blood, like all of 'em. Not Indian, not white, just a mixed-up mess. Don't know where they belong and we don't know where to put 'em." He is right about that—*bad blood*. But why do they have to put us anywhere? There sure isn't gonna be any reservation school in my future. I would just as soon kill myself as go to one of them. God, all those Indians in one place. Real hell. Just let them try to send me. But I look at this empty winter field—no houses, no people except Ange, just snow—and I can see that this place is bad enough.

On my first day at this farm, Ange wakes me up early, making these weird bird noises, "Ooooah oooaheeee," on the steps of her front porch. She tells me that she is praying, but it sounds like strange stuff to me, spells, maybe witchcraft. Then she tells me that she just "spoke" with her mother, Strong Wind, in "Prairie Tongue" and with her father, Jean, in French. Pretending to be asleep, I lie on a knotted rope bed in the corner of a room heated only by a black iron stove spewing smoke and listen to this Indian . . . my grandmother. Her prayers, *li courage miyinauwn*, are called out in even tempo, the rhythm that she seems to move with. She's right about one thing; I sure need it . . . courage, that is.

Once I'm up, I see how carefully planned Angeline's movements are. She tries to draw me into her routine, the first day giving me a bucket and guiding me down a path to some creek. She walks quickly ahead of me, sidestepping branches that snap back and cut my face, but she doesn't laugh when I stumble over the root of a twisted tree in the early morning light. Then she shows me how to draw up a rope pulley thing that she built to bring water from a sinkhole in the deepest part of the creek. I drop the buckets three times because I can't get them to balance right, but finally she helps and we work together until I can do it easily.

After this she leaves me alone so that I can wash myself by the creek's edge, and then protected by the towering red elms on the ridge, pee into the mulberry bushes. Kind of respectful, for an Indian. But when I move back to the water, stepping into a cloud of smoke-colored willows, I see Angeline digging something out of the creek bed. "Skunk cabbage," she tells me. Dirt flying, she paws at the earth. Her right hand now grabs a sharp knife that slices through the thawing mud. Quickly, she cuts the roots from the stems, wrapping each in a piece of worn buffalo hide and placing her weeds in the backpack that she used to bring my snowshoes to the train. Indian stuff, that's all I see. And I'm stuck with it.

Mounds of melting snow flush into the rising creek. This flooded mud bath is Angeline's garden. She works it each morning, hunting down new growth in places I can't even get to. That first morning she puts on her snowshoes and climbs a steep glacier path leading up from the stream. Then she strips narrow ribbons of red bark from some thorny bushes and adds them to her worn-down satchel. I try to follow her, but I slip.

I see that Ange is aware of this, but she doesn't try to help me or speak until we're back on the main path together, crossing the cornfield. Weighed down by the water bucket, I plod along. Angeline's powerful movements challenge me to walk faster. She pushes herself, and eventually so do I. There's no way this old woman is gonna beat me. . . .

When she finally speaks, she begins in French—for both of us, our second tongue—"Ça va, Guillaume?" I search—Joe speaks French. It's there inside of me and I finally answer, "Bien, Ange." Pretending again, I say the truth to myself, "Ça va vraiment terrible."

I want to ask her why she isn't speaking Prairie Tongue, but I don't. Then she's talking like crazy in French about the morning—the snowmelt, her collection of plants that day, and the animals she saw. I get this feeling we're following some other kind of trail, not just this steep slippery path. And I wonder where she's taking me.

"In the late spring, your father, Joe, would swim in this stream. One year he dammed it up so that he could soak his whole body in it." She smiles and the white wrinkles that web the skin around her mouth disappear.

"Did he like to swim?" I'm doing my part to keep this story going, too, hoping she will tell me more. This is still Indian stuff, but hell . . . it is my father. And she sure knew a different Joe than I do.

"Gilles, he looked like *aen kastor*, a large beaver lying in this water," she said. "His hair was shiny red-brown and it would stick straight up, his eyes halfway open just level with the water. He loved to swim here. Beaver medicine was strong in him, Gilles."

A large beaver. So, that's what she sees. But I see Joe, too (I never called him father or dad)—lying at the bottom of the broken stairs in the crumbling Chicago boarding house where we lived, breathing in his own vomit. In my picture, his eyes are closed and he is moaning. Has he hit his head? I remember opening his stained black silk jacket and soft plaid shirt, feeling for his heartbeat. Underneath the whiskey and bile he smells of sweet cloves, the spicy perfume of his tobacco, which I'm always trying to sneak. At his feet, next to a kicked-over bucket, is a diamond-shaped sparkle of glass, a bottle of gin. To me, he looks like a half-dead buffalo.

Ange stops suddenly on the path ahead and is looking back at me. . . . I am worried that she sees my vision. I kneel down beside her to rest my buckets and try not to meet her eyes. Another picture of Joe . . . any would do.

"Ange," I say quickly in French, "Joe and I swam together in the lake. Michigan, one of the giants."

"He told me about swimming in the place where the waters meet the sky, southern sister to the other lakes. It's been many years since I've seen a lake so large."

"Yeah, that's where we would go." *Until he didn't want to get out of bed anymore*, I end this story in my head.

Sensing something—Ange is still looking at me, looking through me—she speaks quietly, "You can lose the *médecine*, Gilles. It can turn around on you. Did it do that for Joe?"

I don't answer her. She knows then. Her son's a drunk Indian. At least, that's what he calls himself in Chicago. What kind of power is that? Shit. I want her to stop looking at me so I can stop thinking about all this. So I decide to shut her up. "Don't you drink, too, Ange? He says it's in your family. In all Indians."

The wrinkles are back, a circle tightening around her mouth guarding her words, her eyes narrowed. She is watching me closely. "I don't have to drink, Gilles. Others do it for me."

By this time we are at the porch, the buckets a quarter empty from my clumsiness in carrying them. After answering me, she walks into her kitchen. Left alone, I feel ashamed. Why did I say that to her? Clumsy, not only with buckets. Joe never blamed her for his drinking. I call her an Indian and she doesn't say anything. She leaves me sitting out there, afraid to go in until a small stream of smoke from the morning train on the horizon reminds me that I'm stuck in this place. I look in the cabin and see her crouched in front of a cookstove, pouring corn-colored liquid into cloudy bottles. Even from the doorway, the heat of the fire singes my face and I feel sweat running down my chest. No chimney in this place, just a furnace. The antiseptic smells of the river plants that we gathered this morning are seeping out of the door.

She doesn't look up when I finally stumble in, but after she hears me coughing on the fumes of her *médecine* from the cookstove, she brings over a small cup of steaming yellow broth.

"Wild mint, pond lily, turkey weed, skunk cabbage—taste it, Gilles," she says in English, holding it to my lips to drink.

I drink slowly, feeling the hot slippery tea coat my tongue, my throat, and finally sink into my stomach. Drinking it, I feel warm and strangely protected. But then I get a queer feeling that she is trying to poison me. . . .

"What's it for, Ange?" I choke it up; piss-yellow liquid spills onto the floor between us.

The silver threads around her face crinkle, her whole face drips with sweat. I feel the heat from the cabin fire building. Sensing fear, she reaches out and touches my hand.

"You want to know, Gilles?" Her hand is cool, stroking my forehead. I realize that she is just a goddamned polite person, and won't say that I'm acting like an ass in any language.

"Hey, Ange, I'm sorry about that stuff I said about drinking."

She shrugs. "Indians drink. For some it is poison. Joe could find it without me."

"Yeah, he did."

She hands me a flask of creek water and then moves to the edge of the porch and sits back on her ankles, rocking slightly. Again, she speaks without looking at me. "Leon always said it to him, Gilles. He called him a drunk Indian."

"Yeah, that's what Joe told me." I don't say what he also mentioned—that she never tried to stop Leon.

We sit like this for a while, Angeline rocking, me drinking the water.

She raises her hand in the air. "*Yootin. Gaitouhtawn.*" (It's windy, I need to go. Come with me). Finally the whispering sounds of the prairie people. Joe had taught me bits and pieces—"The language of dreams," he called it. By switching from our mutually awkward French, she seems to be telling me that she trusts me more now.

Still, I'm not sure I want to go with her, but I don't want to be left alone here, sweating in this scorching cabin thinking about my drunken father. When the social worker guy, Jim, at the orphanage said that I never called him Dad, I told Jim that he never acted like a dad. I was the one always picking him up when he fell, getting us food, and searching for him in dance halls when he wouldn't show up at night. It was never the other way around—the way it was in those Chicago library books. I always knew that Joe cared for me because his hand would grip mine tight before he passed out in those stinking boarding houses. Listening to Ange, I can see him the way she once had—a soaking brown beaver—before whiskey. I remember swimming with him in Michigan. People stopped to watch him swim at the Chicago beach. He propelled himself through the water, stroking so swiftly that when he got out, he would always have an admiring crowd around him. Then he would shake his body hard, showering lake water on the rocks and admiring strangers. He knew how to make them go away, though. He'd slip the diamond-shaped bottle out of the side pocket of his jacket lying in the sand and bite the cork to pull it out, drinking hard before he got dressed. Whenever he bit that cork, the crowd that had been watching backed away. I remember a gentleman shielding his wife's eyes and saying, "Don't look. It's just another Indian, Celeste." I didn't know if Joe heard them, because by that time his eyes were half-closed and he was looking out at the water.

"Come with me, Gilles, if you want."

"Where are we going now?" Ange touches my wrist again; she is still being so polite. Lying on the floor of the porch, I watch her hoist her pack carefully onto her back—where she must have packed the flask into which she had carefully poured the liquid from the stove—and start for the creek path again. She reaches the group of red elms before I catch up with her.

"Are you still thirsty?" she asks, handing me a beaded canteen to fill. She waits on the ridge while I gallop down a gully where the creek pools, pushing my canteen under the water and holding it up to my lips. . . . the water runs down my shirt and soaks me. I fill it again and trudge up the hill. By the time I return she has removed a half-empty glass bottle from her pack, revealing the amber-colored liquid. She instructs me to add creek water from my canteen to fill it. Restocked, she packs it quickly and then sprints down the path.

I race now to keep up with her, and we don't speak until we reach the top of the ridge trail.

"Ange, where are we going?"

"*Mon frayr.*" Her voice lowers when she speaks in Prairie Tongue.

"Your brother lives near here?" I ask.

"Joe never mentioned my brother? He isn't dead." Asking this, her eyes flash a quick something—anger maybe. I had expected to see it when I baited her that morning about the drinking. Nothing then, and now this, but the glint in her eyes disappears quickly.

"About half of his stories were about Red Otter," I finally say. My dad loved this uncle and thought I was like him. I could see it some, all of us named for swimming.

"What stories did he tell you about my brother?"

"Do you want to know, Ange?" This time I ask the question. We are dancing with each other, I think. I let her canteen slip out of my fist and watch it roll down the hill. Clumsy again. She waits while I scramble along the glacier-marbled, rock-infested hillside, slush clumping around my shoes. When I return, she is roping two cabbage-sized dead rabbits onto the bottom of her worn leather bag. Holding and joining their back legs, she fastens them together easily. All this in less time than I took to get the canteen back. I laugh. And so does she. I'm learning to move fast with her, but I'm still the student.

She points to the rabbits on her back. "Red Otter's traps—he sets them well." Turning to look at me, she speaks quietly. "You don't have to protect me from Joe's words. I take care of myself."

"Look, I . . . I know that, Ange."

From her pack, she removes that bottle of golden colored liquid and holds it up to the sun. Speckled pieces of what look like dry leaves float in it.

"What is that stuff?"

"That stuff"—my words sound funny coming from her mouth; she puckers her lips trying to imitate my Chicago slang—"is *la médecine.* 'That stuff' keeps Red Otter alive."

"He's sick?"

"The alcohol from long ago has filled his body, his kidney and liver have been captured, taken over by its spirit. . . . this *l'arb a deend*, turkey weed tea, gives it back to him."

I choke as she sticks the bottle under my nose. It smells worse than Chicago sewer run-off—I could never drink it. Bad, but not as bad as whiskey.

"This is gonna make him better?"

"This will help. Nothing will make him better."

"How did you find out about this?"

"The alcohol spirit sickness or the golden drink? They come together, I think. You don't drink, do you?"

She wanted to hear the truth, so I told her. "I do, Ange."

"Your spirit is still here, but then you are very young."

"I'm not gonna be like my father—some drunk Indian pretending to be French, lying on the floor of a Chicago bar—if that's what you mean."

"Joe didn't want to be a drunk Indian pretending to be French either, Gilles."

The anger is back in her eyes now, but she stops talking and holds her hand up in the air. A wide prairie opens off to our right. To our left, a pattern of farm fields extend along a weaving river. From here I can see the patched fields cut sharply by the knife-straight railroad tracks. She stops moving and we pause at this place for several minutes. I figure she's finally giving me time to rest. Panting, I notice that a small pool of sweat has gathered on her upper lip. She stands and faces a cluster of scrub oak where a cloud of soot-colored ravens flies out of the underbrush and circles over us.

"Strong Wind is here this afternoon, Gilles."

"Strong Wind . . . ?"

"My mother is visiting Red Otter today."

"Your mother is dead."

That's truth, too, but Angeline is no longer listening to me. She is singing in her morning voice to this family of circling crows. Both of her hands are now stretched out above us. She and I are walking very slowly when I hear a deep voice, which seems to come from the dense underbrush, answer her.

"*Ashtum oota, ma soeur* (Come here, my sister)."

"*Tawnshi kiya, mon frayr* (How are you, my brother?)."

"*Li fournoo kishitayw* (The oven is hot, waiting for you)."

"I hope you are waiting for me too, Red Otter, not just your oven."

"I'm always waiting for you, Sister."

Their voices rise together now. "Lord, provide us with direction and understanding." Although I have gotten used to Angeline chanting by herself each morning, hearing her sing with her brother is different. Her voice soars and wraps itself around his, a slow, steady drum in contrast to her birdlike warbles. We enter a grove of river willows, their branches moving above us. Hidden in the shadows ahead, I see a small hut, its walls curved, covered with fog—no, after smelling it, smoke. This thatched structure sprouting birds' nests fascinates me. Drying plants, shedding feathery seeds, hang like low-lying clouds from a willow bark frame hut. I know Indians live in places like this, but seeing it for myself shocks me. The figure inside shocks me even more. His stomach sticks out like a giant pumpkin. This swollen, wrinkled old man with the large orange belly is Red Otter, teller of stories, tamer of horses, and son of Strong Wind. And this guy is my uncle.

Red Otter is lying on a pallet near the opening to his hut, which appears to be constructed of the same willow branches that hang overhead. His doorway is a cramped hole that Angeline and I have to shrink ourselves to fit into. Her pack still on, Angeline kneels down and lays her head across her brother's chest.

His eyes close when she touches him.

He opens his eyes and speaks to me for the first time.

"*Kiya makaw* (How about you), Boy Who Swims?"

He speaks the name that my father first gave me.

Running With the Buffalo

Moments after we arrive, Red Otter opens his prune pit of a mouth so that Ange can empty her whole flask into it. When he swallows the last drops of amber fluid, he opens his mouth this time to speak, and does not close it for my entire visit. He has a mission, sharing tales of the prairie and Red River. He believes that I have been sent to him for this purpose, and he is relentless in his pursuit of it. My grandmother talks, too, but she is far less the storyteller. It is already clear to me that her life is revealed in her actions, not in her words.

Angeline swiftly unfolds a wrapped buckskin package, covered with pine needles and winterberries, from her pack and draws out a long straight needle. She then plunges the needle straight into Red Otter's pumpkin-shaped belly. Pink fluid, the color of the early morning sunrise, shoots up, hitting her face. She spits it out of her mouth and Red Otter groans. They begin chanting *Not cretoer, li courage miuauwn* (Our creator, give us courage). She pulls out a second needle and sticks it into the other side of his giant belly. Within minutes the pumpkin disappears, and Red Otter's stomach returns to nearly normal size, a small mound covered in deerskin hugging his ribs. Then, Angeline swiftly removes each of the needles and reaches again into her skin pouch to pull out a paper-wrapped packet of a salve, smelling sharply of ammonia, which she gently massages into the two wounds. They are chanting through all of it.

She reaches for my thumbs and places them in the slippery ointment over the now oozing holes. What would come out of these holes if I stopped?

For the first time since she began, Red Otter opens his smoke-colored eyes and smiles. "Boy Who Swims, finally you have come to join us." I want to tell him that I'm not a boy, not Boy Who Swims, not any boy. I am Gilles, and already, at almost sixteen, I have lived a man's life. But instead I am quiet, and push my thumbs hard into his stomach. Why is Ange having me do this? Lying only inches from his chest, I can see and feel that his breathing is becoming regular. His ribs push out farther with each breath. He is breathing strong now, but I wonder what would happen if I disagreed with him, tell him I'm Gilles, not Boy Who Swims. That would probably kill him. So I say nothing.

He doesn't seem to mind that I'm not talking. He has plenty to tell me. It is probably better that I am quiet. No interruptions that way.

"Bird With First Snow tells me that they tried to send you to one of those reservation schools to assist you with your education. You didn't go, did you?"

I shake my head, but Red Otter's eyes close again, and I'm not sure he has seen me. He must feel my head move, though, because his voice drops to a whisper. "They sent me to one. Sure, I learned there. That's where I first learned about the poison."

With this effort his voice cracks and he starts hacking, a rasping non-stop noise. Something deep in his chest. I don't want him to die, not here with me. Ange comes over and places her hand on his neck. His throat muscles tighten and I hear tiny gasps—is he still breathing? Is he gonna die because I was pushing too hard on his stomach? Angeline moves a smooth flat rock under the back of his neck, massages his throat, and gently moves my thumbs away. The coughing stops, and he slowly goes on with his story, mixing French and Prairie Tongue.

"That school they sent me to was between here and Red River, a stone monument, built in the land of the Chippewas. They promised us an education, and that's what they gave us. Before you can get 'educated' though, they have to take something away. So that's what they did. First, they took away our language, our Prairie Tongue. We had to use their words, English. On Sunday, they would be kind to us. We could speak French or English, but still no prairie words. It was a Christian school, after all. French and English, they are the Christian languages. Prairie Tongue was for heathens. The teachers threatened to cut out the tongues of the boys who couldn't stop using the prairie words. A couple kids didn't catch on. They left them their tongues, but beat them until they couldn't speak . . . they could only scream. Michael Long Elk yelled the loudest. He couldn't learn any language except Prairie Tongue and he hardly knew that, not a word at all until he turned eight. He was Cree, a cousin of my mother, Strong Wind. She was the one who taught him the few words that he knew. She started with the animals—buffalo, wild deer, weasel, wolf. He learned them all. Then she taught him the words for food—corn, wild berries, prairie dog stew. But that was all he could say. We told them that. The teachers thought he was making fun of them—rebelling, they said. I offered to teach Michael. Just tell me the English words for animals, that's all I asked them for. That night, they beat me too, long red stripes appeared on my shoulders. They beat Michael Long Elk until he stopped screaming and spit up blood. He died late that night. After he died, we made a circle around him and held hands while Michael joined with the spirits.

"The next day was Sunday, so at first we sang his death chant in French. Then we moved into our own words, Prairie Tongue, singing how we wanted to beat their backs until they bled to death, pull out their tongues if they didn't speak the right words. It was that day when we realized that the French brother at our school, le Père Norbet, was deaf in one ear, probably hit on the head when he was sent to Christian School. He could not tell what we were saying, so we told him we were chanting old French, not Prairie Tongue, that we were singing for Michael, the language of the hearty woodsmen, *les coureurs de bois*, our French fathers and grandfathers. Hearing this, the brother joined in our chant, tapping his buckled shoe and smashing his enormous fist down on the table where Michael's body was lying so hard that his body started bouncing up and down. This priest was from the south of France, and spoke his *oui*'s with a whisper. We told him that our song was different because our grandfathers were from the north—Nancy, brave men with vintage accents. Then, the oldest boy there, White Cloud, remembered the antelope dance. He led us in a line around the table where Long Elk was lying. At first we danced slowly, then our legs pounded up and down. With our heads thrust forward, we began to move like antelope. We left that school. We were crossing the plains. Just north of Red River, a herd of buffalo was alongside us. Every once in a while we would shout a French word, and the old curate would nod his head, *une grande chanson, mes garcons, chantez plus fort*, a great song, my boys, sing louder. That day, we were no longer half-breed boys in a reservation school. We were young bucks running with the buffalo."

Red Otter's eyes are wide open by the time he finishes. His own story has charged him up. I can see that he is anxiously looking around for Ange, because he relaxes when she is near him.

"Quiet. Rest while the rabbits are cooking, Little Brother. Boy Who Swims will stay for a while," Ange whispers in Prairie Tongue.

"He will stay, but I am not going to, even with your wise bird medicine."

"You don't know that, Brother."

I see his eyes meet hers as he answers, "I do know that, my sister. When does Man Who Sings With Hands return?"

"Leon will stay until the state legislature closes for planting. He has no desire to return early."

"He is a fool, sister."

"I must check the fire. Tell him about our father."

Red Otter is ready to do just that. He steadies his hands at his side and pulls himself up until he is nearly sitting upright. Suddenly I realize he is tall, a head taller than Angeline, even taller than me, cross-legged on the floor beside him. I want to ask him a question, but he is staring off, back in the land of the Chippewas, the neighbors of the Métis. He gets me thinking about that other school, my school, the Chicago orphanage, no boys doing antelope dances there. They speak the language of the streets, not the prairie. Like Red Otter, I still have dreams about my education.

"Boy Who Swims, where are you now?" Red Otter asks in a gentle voice, but I feel his eyes enter me, looking for something.

"What's your story?" he asks again.

I shrug. "I don't have any."

He laughs. "You mean you don't want to tell any."

"Yeah, I don't want to tell. Won't make it any easier."

"No, probably not."

I know that it won't really make it any easier, but the urge to tell is pushing on my throat and I open my mouth and tell him my story.

My first night at the orphanage the policemen handed me over to the director, a tall man in gray overalls. He wasted two or three minutes with me, then shoved me into a room with a group of other boys. At twelve, I was probably the youngest, but I was already tall like you. The director winked at another tall boy called Jared who was wearing a jacket with a fur collar, a rich kid's jacket, strange apparel in this jail for kids. The man clicked the door handle loudly when he left. When I moved to a cot and put my pack down, Jared shouted at me, "You crazy, boy? The Indians sleep over there, not in here with us." He pointed at the floor in the corner.

I turned and started to walk out of the dormitory room, knowing that the boys were staring at my back. I knew that the other kids were scared, too. They watched and said nothing when strong-armed and rough-mouthed Jared shoved me to the floor and called me "redface." I didn't fight with him. Instead, I picked myself and my suitcase up and walked out of the room, not knowing where I was going. I just hoped that Jared wouldn't follow me. And I didn't want to meet up with that director, McDermott, again. When that man looked at me, I felt like he saw part of the dirty snow covering the Chicago streets, snow that he had a godly mission to get rid of. It didn't matter that his words were sweet, promising me education—just what kind of education did he mean? Joe had told me about these kind of places—"Don't get stuck in one of those, Gilles. They don't care about kids. They've just got to have a place to lock them up so they don't have to look at them on the streets." Late one night, Joe had told me about what they did to Indian kids at those places. He wasn't there to help me, though.

When I left the room, I closed the door softly, not like the heavy shove of the night supervisor in his over-large striped overalls, and looked up and down the long hall that ran across the top story of the orphanage. I knew that if I were found out of my room bad things would happen—I had to find a place to hide quick. I walked about halfway down the hall before I found a door and entered a closet that felt like it was filled with tools. My foot landed in a bucket half-filled with water. I closed the door, and aided by a cloud of light that crept under it, I wedged a mop across it. Neither Jared nor anyone else was going to find me that night.

Huddled in the janitor's closet, I heard cries from the dormitory. Jared hadn't found me, but he wasn't alone that night. I covered my ears and thought of my father. Just where was he now? I remembered seeing him crumpled at the bottom of the steep stairs of the boarding house where we lived. His eyes were closed, and he was moaning. I was worried that he may have hit his head too hard. When I felt his heart, it was beating and he was still breathing. Reaching under him, I felt the empty bottle of whiskey at his side. Of course, he was drunk, and he had probably fallen down the stairs. I ran out the front door looking for help. A few minutes later, the police arrived. I asked them for help. They grabbed my shoulder and pushed me against the hall, "Kid, show us your sick father." I felt their rough grip and smelled their sour breath when they pressed their faces close to me. Not knowing what to do, I took them down the backstairs to show them where he had been lying. He wasn't there. The two police looked at me in disbelief. They had to turn in somebody, so still gripping my arm they brought me to McDermott's boys' orphanage, a sooty brick building with bars halfway up its windows. McDermott's social worker told me the bars were there because they didn't want anyone to break in and hurt the kids, but I knew the real reason. No boys escaped, and the bars hid the crimes that were taking place here. That social worker guy, Jim, had a nice face, but I was pretty sure that he didn't have a clue about what was happening.

In the closet, I considered my choices. I wasn't going back to that dormitory with Jared and the boys. Remembering Jared's bloodshot eyes and the younger boys' scared faces, I knew it was a private hell. What to do? I recalled several gates—wooden, steel. This place wouldn't be easy to get out of.

An hour, maybe two passed. I felt my stomach tighten with hunger. Even here, there had to be a kitchen. Maybe I could find it. I had helped my dad cook for restaurants. Maybe the cook would let me stay there, and I wouldn't have to return upstairs to Jared. Maybe. It took me a while to discover a foul-smelling greasy kitchen in a cold basement, but the cook did let me sleep there in return for waking up early to help him. And, with his help, I left with the baker in his truck after breakfast, bribing him with an offer to lift his heavy delivery out of the truck. I was stuck in the back with rich people's bread, the stuff they never left for orphans. But, I got out. Red Otter didn't. My uncle was "educated" in that school for five years. Sitting next to him, I feel like his story counts more than mine. In mine, boys just got screwed, but in his, they are beaten, even killed. Yeah, his is a worse lot, but at least he got to run with the buffalo.

Leon Returns

*E*very morning for the next month, I follow Angeline up the Ridge trail to Red Otter's home, just after the sun approaches the cornfield. We are joined by the nose-watering smells of her early morning tea—sugar mint, pine needles, and skunk cabbage—which cling to our clothes for most of our walk. She carries her buffalo bag, stopping to collect leaves, berries, rocks, even dirt—sometimes telling me in Prairie Tongue what she is doing. But mostly we're quiet. After we get to Red Otter's, she works in his hut chopping, grinding, and mixing her morning harvest. Clay jars of medicines line the elm wood shelves that enclose his room. For hours, Angeline crouches over his small metal stove, boiling strong-smelling liquids that she pours into carefully saved glass bottles.

Red Otter can walk the day after our first visit, and squats outside his hut when Ange is working, unless she asks him to bring her something. I usually sit with him, listening to his stories, but I also want to be inside with her. I have gotten used to the pungent smells by now and am more than a little curious about what she is making. Red Otter tells me that their mother, Strong Wind, was a powerful healer who taught Angeline many of her chants and a lot about *les médecines*, but that his sister's healing touch is special. After I see her stick those needles in Red Otter's stomach, I believe in it, too. I want to know how she makes her medicine, but then again, after pushing my thumbs into my uncle's bloody holes, I feel like I need to be with him, watching him breathe. I keep thinking he might die at any moment. But I also get something. My uncle knows stories about a lot more than buffaloes and his musical voice is always singing his words in French. Sometimes I ask him a question, but mostly I don't have to. Different from Ange, he almost always speaks in English or French, confiding that he is saving Prairie Tongue for his sister to teach me. Joe uses it, too, but mostly when he is drunk, mixing it in with his French. English, Joe saves for his few sober moments. But even though Red Otter doesn't speak Prairie Tongue with me, he's the one who tells me how it works.

"Plant, sew, hunt—the work words, Gilles, are usually in Cree, the language of our mother. Things, though, that's different, especially things anyone owns—furs, carts, horses. Those words are always in French. It's a trade, kind of like a marriage."

"French own all the stuff? That doesn't seem fair to me."

"It isn't, but that's the way the language grew." Then he adds, "When Strong Wind and my father spoke the words together, there was music to it. She was Cree, the language joined their lives. They each still had something—not like the schools. When the teachers spoke with you there, that was no marriage. They took your song, then they took everything else and made you forget you had ever had it."

He is right. It was a trade. But I could see that even in language, the trade wasn't even.

I ask Ange about it when we are walking home that evening. At first, she doesn't want to talk, but after I tell her Red Otter's buffalo dance story, her eyes begin to water. She doesn't say anything for a long time. She just stops walking and stands calmly until her tears cease. I wait.

"After he was sent home from school, my brother didn't say anything—no English, no French, no Prairie Tongue. Many of the others died at school—the beatings, the food, the poison liquor, the fevers—but not Red Otter, not my strong brother who was born in the year of the great prairie fire. Boys born that year were stronger than others. He just didn't talk for a year. He lost his singing voice. They might as well have cut out his tongue. "

A year? He, a man of many stories, had been a boy who stopped speaking for a year.

"Then they sent him home to you?"

"Yes. I tried to cure him of the poison in his blood—you see all my drinks. But nothing cures that, Gilles."

She is walking again, but more slowly. Behind her now, I notice a rough ribbon of gray woven into her long brown braid. First her brother, then her son, my father—booze took them both.

"I tried to cure my dad, too, Ange. I poured water into his whiskey bottles."

She does not look back, but when she speaks her shoulders move slightly upward, and she seems less burdened.

"I know you did, Gilles. With your father it was different than with Red Otter. First, he wanted to have possessions he couldn't have. Then he wanted to be what he wasn't. They didn't take his tongue. They convinced him he wanted a different one. There were lots of things that he wanted to be different, Gilles, things that I couldn't make up to him, ever."

I know what she is talking about, not only with my father, but with the boys I saw at the orphanage. They were always looking out through the barred windows at the Chicago streets, their eyes glued to tall, proud white men on over-groomed horses, or muscled white delivery men hauling cumbersome boxes into carts, even sleepy white farmers delivering washed vegetables to market. They saw and wanted it all. Joe desires a lot of things too—silver tie clips, diamond cuff links, imported French suits, and the highest quality Prohibition whiskey. When he can't get the things he wishes for, he lives only in his drunken dreams. I know that I'm not so different from him or the others. I look out of the same starved eyes as the other boys. I want that stuff, too. Ange might understand how I feel, but I'm not sure whether I can tell her. I'm worried that I'll just become another problem in her life, one that she will have to create potions and prayers for. So, I decide not to tell her.

I come to this resolution just as we reach the top of Dead Squirrel Hill, the highest point on the Ridge Trail between Red Otter's and Ange's homes. Ange tells me it was so named because both the squirrels and the dead congregate there. That's who the chattering squirrels are speaking with when we get there. Looking down from this rock-covered cliff above Ange's farmhouse, I see the young corn shoots stretching out around it, reaching from White Oak Creek all the way down to the train tracks. It is from up there that I see a dot of a man cutting a diagonal path through the center of the largest cornfield. Ange and I always walk along the edges of any field, to avoid any trampling of growing plants. We watch as his shape grows larger, more distinct. The way this man is marching straight through, I know that he is leaving a wide-open trail of mashed seedlings behind him. I notice that although he tramps hard and strong, he has an uneven step and shifts his weight back and forth between his hips, his left foot making a circular dance every time he brings it forward. Even from the ridge, it is clear that his physical movements demand a great deal of energy, each step punctuated by a thrusting chest. His lungs expand like bellows as he lurches forward, marking his walk with loon-like cries that chase the ground animals out of the way. Watching him cross a quarter of the field, I see that he walks with this rolling gait, his hip jutting out, because his wiry right leg is inches shorter than his left. I feel like he is stealing my energy just to move himself forward. Exhausted, I try to look away. But, for some reason I just can't stop staring at his face. The closer he moves, the more I try to pull my eyes away. I see a pair of snarling black eyebrows framing light, almost translucent, otherworldly, blue eyes, eyes too peaceful for that grimacing face.

Angeline sees him, too. Her face is shaded by one of the brush elms, but she has stopped walking and is also tracking his progress. As he comes closer, I notice that he is shoeless. Over-polished, tied together and slung on his right shoulder, his shoes bounce with every step. In his left hand he carries a paddle-shaped leather case hugged protectively close to his body so that it doesn't bounce as much as the rest of him. Ange and I stand quietly watching him for several more minutes, until he arrives at the front steps of the house. He places the leather case carefully on the steps and brushes the dust from his coat.

I guess it. Leon is home. Angeline waits until he disappears inside the house before she breaks into a run, knocking stones off the ridge in her hurry to get to him. After stopping to fill the water buckets, I follow her up the creek path.

The Metal Cross

*S*liding in the aftermath of the sandy gravel avalanche that Ange kicks up after she takes off down the ridge, I have more than enough time to remember the only thing that Joe told me about his father. When I asked, he said simply that Leon was carrying a heavy burden. My father, being an educated man, probably understands that some people might associate this to White Man's Burden because, after all, Leon claims he is a white man, a white man living with a bunch of Indians and half-breeds. A white man in his own view. Leon looks white . . . albino white, china-baby white, noon-day cloud white. But I know Joe wasn't talking about White Man's Burden when he talked about Leon. No manifest destiny, no living with, caring for, and educating those whom he considers less fortunate than himself, none of that is for Leon. Yet, Joe saw it clearly. Leon is carrying something.

From my place perched on the ridge, I look to the open door of the cabin and I see that Leon is also a hungry man. Apart from his lake-colored eyes, it is raw cannibalism I see in his face. Leon is eating himself up. He is an angry man. It changes the way things feel around him. I don't even have to look at his thrusting chest or listen to his scary cries to feel the violence that my father described in his stories of him. But it is even more than that, just watching him, Leon's anger travels deep into my gut and begins gnawing. Animals can get out of his way, but for me there is no escape. Already, his anger starts to make a home in my body. I have to work hard to keep my chest from thrusting out like his. Exhausted, I sit in the dirt. Even from here, I can see Ange running to the front door of the cabin. I watch Leon step out of the house and stand on the porch waiting. For a moment, I see some of the anger drain out of his face. His jaw is still twisted, but his chest is spasming less now. They stop short of each other, and his cheek presses toward hers. But then nothing happens. They don't touch. I have to look away. Walking slowly toward the house I find the leather-covered bundle of herbs that Ange dropped in her rush to get to Leon, and stuff a fallen pond lily clinging to clumps of soft wet mud back in her pack.

Getting closer, I see Leon give Ange a small, square package wrapped in crinkled paper and sealed with a splattered red flower mark of wax. She struggles to unwrap it, trying not to break its seal. She strokes it, turning it over and over, searching for a way to avoid ripping it, but she is too slow for Leon. Smile gone, left cheek twitching madly, he is watching her, too, and wants her to open it. He has brought this goddamn present all the way from Springfield, and now she is just staring at the thing. "Open it, just open it, Ange." His heavily French-accented English attacks my ears as I approach them. With a single motion, his right arm moves across her stomach and pops the seal, which shoots it into the air. Paper tissue floats to Angeline's feet, leaving her holding a silver cross hanging from a wide-linked chain. From my position above them I can see that she doesn't know what to do with it. She is holding it, but staring off at something else. Then I see that her half-closed eyes have found the crimson wax blossom, still intact, at the edge of the field—the seal. Quickly she kneels and grabs for it.

Leon shouts in French, "Put it on." She turns and stares at him, the cross in one hand, the seal in the other. Still, she does nothing.

Again he speaks. "The cross! I want to see you wear it. Put it on."

She doesn't move, and he grabs the cross from her hand, twisting the chain as he pulls it up to encircle her neck. But she says nothing, her eyes still focusing on the seal in her open palm.

By the time I make it up to them and drop Ange's buffalo pack on the porch, they are locked arm against arm, Leon twisting the chain of the clasp around her neck as he tightens it. Her eyes, still half-closed, are fixed on the red badge in her hand. She isn't fighting him. Caught up, they don't see me standing there, watching, and so I wait for several moments, trying not to look even though I see him pressing her back hard against his chest. Then, a distant train whistle blows. It startles Leon and his arm jerks across Ange's chest, pushing the silver cross up against her right breast. Her eyes are now completely closed. They stand frozen. Then Leon turns and notices me. He drops his hand and lets go of her.

"What's he doing here, Ange?" He sputters French words.

"He has been with me since the train arrived at noon." She is matter-of-fact, and does not mention that the train arrived several months before.

Leon closes his eyes now. "He can't stay here."

"Because you don't want him, Leon?"

Now, it takes him a while to answer. I look at his eyes and see that he is searching for something "factual," that he doesn't want to say the truth . . . his truth. "It's about what's good for the boy. . . . Ange, it ain't good for him being here." I wonder why this guy doesn't look at me. Is this the way he treated my dad?

"You know this?" She now turns to face him.

"He's got to go to school. Stuck out here with you—it won't happen for him." Her eyes can no longer meet his directly and are focused on his jerking arm.

"So we send him to that Indian orphanage? Leon, that's the 'school' they're talking about, a place where they'll teach him to hate himself."

Leon looks away. His cheek is twitching again, but his voice is low and even. He has regained his self-control and is trying to convince her.

"Ange, I don't know what to do. I can try to talk to some people in Springfield. There have got to be other places. He can't stay here. It's not right for him."

Ange puts her hand up, trying to stop his words.

"You mean it's not right for you. We're talking about him just like we talked about Joe."

"Don't bring that up, Ange. It was different with Joe. He should have been here."

"With you?"

"What are you saying? That I should leave . . . ? So that you can raise him alone?"

"I'm not saying that, Leon. I'm not saying that."

I wonder what she is trying to say. I know that she doesn't want me to go. But what is she saying to him? Even to me, it isn't clear. It is, however, my first observation of the dance that Angeline does with Leon, and I take it in, hating it.

Jigging

*T*hings change right after Leon arrives. Ange and I no longer spend our days with Red Otter at Willow Grove. She visits him before I'm awake now. After her return, we crowd into the cornfield cabin where Leon occupies the center of the room in an oak rocker that twitches in rhythm with his face. It is hard not to look at him. Ange, in contrast, squats by her wood stove, blending so well with the hanging herbs and smells of her medicines that she seems invisible. I pretend to read, but most of the time I'm watching them or dreaming about Chicago streets. After the first day, I don't hear them talk about me, but I imagine I'm still on their minds. For me, it is hard not to think about my situation. Hours go by as Ange cooks and Leon rocks, speaking only to Ange. Some days we all work together out in the cornfields. There, Ange gives the orders and Leon seems easy about doing what she asks. The tension drops from his face, and I begin to feel like we might be a family. I even think about staying here for good.

A month after he is home, Leon hitches up their charette, a relic used for carrying carcasses during the buffalo days, and drives us five miles into Ashkomb. He tells Ange and me to ride on top with him. When we get about a mile out of Ashkomb, he starts talking about Red River. Why is this happening today? Until that moment, Leon hasn't said more than a hundred words to Ange or me. According to Leon, Red River is a place north of the Canadian border, an outpost where the wind and wolves howl all night, even in the heat of summer. When I ask him about the buffalo, he tells me that they should be shot. Any that are still left alive, that is. For him, Red River is a wild place that has to be tamed. And he believes that everything happens for a reason, even the killing. Keeping this in mind, I realize that his sudden talking also has a purpose. He spouts off a piece of a bragging conversation he has had with the governor . . . he cares about the colony . . . and he listens to me. Hard for me to believe that anybody could care about this podunk place, a backwater town overcrowded with Métis and American relations, almost all half-breeds.

By the time we arrive at the courthouse, I'm beginning to get Leon. I see that the time has come for him to run for his state assembly seat and so, run he is, moving from five to five thousand words a day— French, English, Métis, Cree. Leon is speaking them all and faster than anyone I've ever heard. But I realize that he is speaking solely for the purpose of winning votes. Later that afternoon, when he gets tired of talking, or more likely when others are tired of listening, he opens up the paddle-shaped package that I saw him bring from the train and uses this other voice, his Red River fiddle, to woo his constituents, playing on the courthouse stairs. Even Red Otter, who believes the colony is better off when the assembly is in session and Leon is living in Springfield, concedes that Leon is the finest fiddler in the colony and that Leon wins his elections not by word, but by song.

When Leon opens his worn felt case, steadies his short legs on a box, picks up his homemade bow, tilts his trembling chin and plucks his first notes, the music swells into the corners of any room and everyone is up. *Tap, tap, tap* . . . Even my left foot starts moving and my right hand reaches for an imaginary partner. I want to pick up a bow and join him, and what's more, his songs make me believe I can.

Fiddling, Leon replaces with sweet pleasures the sharp pains that he causes in others. I notice that Ange is finally smiling. Leon's songs also carry the sacred memories of Red River.

How does it work, that a man who seemed as unable to feel as Leon, can bring out the strongest passions in others? I tell myself, he must be feeling something to do this. When I ask Red Otter, who has been sitting and watching, he rambles about Leon's dark passion—his anger—alerting me to how easily one can be sucked into it. "I don't know" is what he says about Leon's talent for bringing music to others, but adds that Leon's father has run with the buffalo, as if that explains all. At one of these indoor jigging campaigns, I sense what it must have been like to live in Red River. I see that it is a nation of foot-tappers, if this colony is any indication. The older folks begin the dancing, their feet barely leaving the dirt floor of the barn, but their movements are so fast my eyes cross trying to keep up. Angeline and Red Otter, who had been carried to the hall on his willow pallet, stand and dance side-by-side, mirroring each other's steps before they split off, each heading a line. No jig, this dance, but everyone follows easily, girls and women behind Ange, the men trailing after Red Otter. Weaving side to side, each leads a procession that finally joins together back at Leon with a double circle, men in the middle. Then the two lines pair off again, but this time men and women partner with each other. I noticed that Leon signals these switches with three quick jerks of his bow and a shout, "O ye yaille." Miraculously, the dancers seem to know exactly what to do at these moments—either partnering in two's, revealing intricate patterns of interlocking arms and feet, a dance where the couple has to know where their partners are at all times, or the floor clears and all join a weaving line that reminds me of Red Otter's story with the buffalo—animals and people wind across an infinite space. Lying on the floor where Leon has told me to go—"Don't make a fool of ourself, Gilles"—with those who are neither children nor adults, les jeunes sophisticates, I take it all in. I feel my body rise up and join the dancers. Why did my dad leave this place for those Chicago dives? Diamond cuff links, French suits, and even blended whiskey doesn't explain it.

Spread out, propped up against a wall, I see Marie-Thérèse for the first time. It is her legs that I notice first, flashes of bare skin encased in a sweeping black skirt and varied shades of dusky blue petticoats. Those flashes of deep cobalt silk draw my eyes to Marie-Thérèse, at least to her legs, for she is kicking higher than any of the other girls or women. She has this star shuffle pattern down, but it is the tiny thrust that she adds at the end of each set that has everyone staring. Sometimes, she kicks forward, a couple times, then I see her kick back, her boots clicking together as she shouts "Et tu, Léon," after he lets out a sharp cry to punctuate his fiddling. Lying there, watching, I imagine that I have seen this kicking woman before, but I can't figure out where. Fantasy lady, I know I want this to be true, but I think I'm dreaming. Then, it comes to me.

My father's pocket watch has a place for only one photograph, and in it a young Marie-Thérèse, maybe seven years old, rests in my mother's arms. She is my mother's half-sister. This is the photo that I'd stare at when my father was drunk and I was trying to pry him off the floor. The photo, an unusual pose for the time it was taken, is different from the tight-lipped non-touching photos of family members lined up in Victorian dresses by other traveling photographers. In this sepia image the two sisters dress in white blouses, dark skirts, and woven Métis sashes, and embrace. Marie-Thérèse looks up at my mother's face, her full lips pursed as if she has just kissed or been kissed. Whenever I gaze at their faces, I guess that the photographer has intruded on something that should have been kept private.

Lying there, eyes closed, I understand it is Marie-Thérèse's portrait that causes the odd feeling I have about the photo. Her face stays with me, her arched neck, gently curved cheeks and pouting lips. My mother, who is staring straight ahead in the traditional Victorian manner, seems not to notice the obvious sentiments emanating from her younger sister. Lying on the floor of the crowded jigging hall, I open my eyes to see Marie-Thérèse's mouth.

She is standing over me, her lips parted to speak. "*Et tu, Gilles, le fils de Madeline, finalement, ahh.*" (And you, Gilles, Madeline's son, finally.)

After greeting me, she kneels on the floor, close-by, coils back her head, rocks side to side, moving to Leon's music which has slowed in tempo. The dancers are streaming around us, but I feel alone with her, like I've awakened in my father's photograph. This close, I know why I've always stared at her face when I open that watch. Yeah, I've looked at my mother's face, but judged her far-off gaze as that of a dreamer, living mostly in her head. It's this face I'm keenly drawn to. Where is my loyalty? My mother dead, and I her only child. In Joe's locket, Marie-Thérèse is only a girl lying in her sister's arms . . . but spread out on this barn floor—ohh! Her pursed lips, now inches from mine, are only the beginning. Her face glows. On her ears she wears tiny gold rings that sparkle with sweat brought on by the hard dancing and packed bodies, and I notice that she, like Angeline, puts out a strong smell. Hers isn't some medicinal nose cleaner. Instead, I smell an unrecognizable perfume, a strong hypnotic that makes me want to press my face into her hair.

Marie-Thérèse is studying my half-closed eyes carefully. I wonder if she has guessed the effect that she is having on me. If she knows, I curse her. My arms and back are now welded to the floor, immobilized. I am stiffening inside my pants, but in an entirely different way from my upper part—I'm angry; she has drugged me into becoming a cripple. Now she is offering me a cup of cloved wine, which she sips along with me. Whether or not she is doing this purposefully, I still want to kill her, but I am paralyzed, lying flat on my back, mesmerized by soft words which are capturing more than my attention, and have now plunged my lower part into crippling spasms. Different from the languages spoken by Ange, Red Otter, or even Leon, I see Marie speaks her own tongue. And I'm not sure what it is. All I know is that I can listen to her for hours, even though I'm not sure what she is saying.

Marie-Thérèse does not seem to notice that I do not understand her. She speaks, I smile. She nods, I nod. We are communicating quite well, or so I think. Then she abruptly leaves. Has she seen? She comes back with a pancake covered with small raisins and powdered sugar.

"*Les kreps, Gilles, watausch pahminnan.*" I smile again, and she nods again. Then she starts filling my mouth with pancakes, dusting my lap with sugar, outlining the shape that I'm trying so hard to hide. She spills the goddamn sugar across her dark blouse where it outlines her breasts, shapes I both do and do not want to look at. Half-juiced and more than half-hard, the victim of her sweet wine, I have to do something—fast. Then, the fiddle starts again and I stand up, pulling her along with me. This jig is quick, too quick for me to follow, but Marie-Thérèse moves her feet swiftly and slides out of the way of my heavy-muddied boots.

"*Tu danses comme ton père, Gilles.*"

Is this a compliment? Yes. No. Maybe. All I know is that I am not as hard as I have been, and the spasms are stopping now. My body's back under my control—barely. Marie-Thérèse is looking down, staring right at it, I am sure. Serves her right, if she sees it. Slowly, I realize that it is my feet she is looking at, trying to match her steps to mine. She is saying words that I can't understand. Maybe she doesn't even know what is going on with me.

I keep watching her jumping black boots . . . right, back, left, kick. Then, it kind of happens. We are dancing. I can do it . . . right, back, left, kick. I look up. The music stops, but Thérèse and I are still moving, her arms gripping my shoulders. No one is watching. Then I see that this is not exactly true; on the raised stage, half a field away, I see Leon, his bow in the air and his eyes on us. I stumble and nearly fall, but Thérèse saves me by twisting her body around mine, pressing her damp silk shirt against my arm. I don't look, but I know that Leon is watching us. My stomach hurts and I think, "I'm going to puke." I lean over, feeling pulled to the floor, but she touches my back. When I look up I realize that Thérèse's lips are moving. "Gilles, let's go. We do not have to stay here. Come with me."

I know that he is staring at us as she puts her moist hand in mine and leads me out of the dance hall. I don't look back. In fact, I can't even look at the dancers that we're bumping into, afraid they are watching and judging me, too. Once we are outside, I breathe deeply and can see again, this time outlines of the oversized wagons and animal shadows, highlighted by burning torches. I drop her arm, trying to push away its soft cool caress that brings back feelings I am trying to get rid of. She doesn't touch me again, but walks over to one of the huge charettes, parked by the river, and leans back, her small body framed by its huge wooden wheel.

"Gilles, he is not here watching us."

So, she too had felt his gaze.

"It doesn't matter, Thérèse, I still feel him." Saying her name for the first time makes me glow.

She nods but doesn't answer me. We stay like that for at least an hour, staring at the Illinois. A warm river mist rising from the night water hovers around us. I'm not hard anymore, but I feel like doing something . . . putting my arm around her, or lifting her into the wagon and licking the sweat on her upper lip. I don't.

Rebellion

*L*eon slaps the scarred left flank of Annie le Rouget, our oldest draft horse, as Ange and I climb into the charette. Ange's eyes startle but Le Rouget doesn't jump, waiting patiently until we've piled into the creaking cart. Then, amazingly, we're moving very fast through clouds of swirling white fog. The night air is still warm, but it is being infused with cool river mist, which I see condensing on the hairs of Angeline's hand now resting on mine. We are galloping, unsteadily pitching our path in the muddy streets as we weave our way to the farmland road. No one speaks. Instead, we listen to the snap of the whip against the horse's skin.

Leon is quiet until we cross our farm's front acres of newly sprouted corn.

"Gilles, *cette coquine* is your aunt. How could you not know? What were you thinking?" He spits the words at me.

"We were dancing," I say, but think, *Why do I make excuses to him?*

"They watch you. How you act is important here. I want you to understand that." His hand tightens on the whip.

I look into the mist now settling over the growing corn shoots, searching for an escape from his tight, angry voice. . . . *How could I not know? What does it matter? And why does he have to scream it out loud?*

"I understand," I answer in a level voice. The air feels wet, soaking my lungs as I breathe in deeply and close my eyes. . . . *Just don't fight with him, I caution myself. We are almost home. . . . I'll put the horses in the barn and sleep with them. Then, I'll think about this in the morning.*

"Leon," Ange is speaking now, "Gilles and I understand that how we act is important for you, but Marie-Thérèse is not what you called her. She is Elisabeth's daughter, and the sister of Gilles's mother."

"She is more than that. She flashes her legs and breasts at her young nephew and then leaves the dance with him. Everyone is watching, and they are not so kind with their words."

"You are the one who is not kind."

"You choose to spend your time with the Junots. Those women are whores . . . Indian—" At this, his voice crackles.

"—Indian whores, Leon? Is that what you were going to say? Indian whores, like me?"

"Look, Ange. That isn't what I said. Anyway, Gilles doesn't need to hear this. You are shaming yourself in front of the boy."

"It doesn't matter what you say, if that's what you're thinking inside." For once she seems totally focused on Leon, oblivious to me.

"People are watching us closely here. We have to act a certain way."

Leon goes on for what seems like hours. I know that Ange can manage him, but I'm getting sick of listening.

"Just what 'certain ways' are you talking about, Leon?" I hear my own voice.

"Gilles, you stay out of this," he snaps.

"I'm already in it. I just haven't said anything yet."

"Look, I'm saying that when you and Marie-Thérèse left the hall, there was talk."

"What kind of talk do you mean, Leon?" I can feel a growing nausea in my stomach, and know that I am not going to let up on him. So many months of silent anger. "Just what were they saying, Leon, that Marie-Thérèse was taking me down to the river to do me . . . or were they saying that I was gonna do her? Or maybe it wasn't exactly like that? Maybe it was more like what you said—that we're two Indians. Not a name to call your grandson, huh? 'Course you're not really Indian, are you Leon? Your blood is pure."

"I told you to stay out of this!"

"But Leon, in your mind I'm already in it. What I wonder is what you were thinking Marie-Thérèse and I were doing . . . 'cause it's gotta be a whole lot worse than anything that was actually going on back there at the river. I'd rather have the whiskey-saturated blood of a dying race in my veins than your pure shit. . . ."

Crack. I hear it before I see it. Leon has moved the whip off the horses' backs and brought it down hard on mine. Biting my lip, I ignore the pain and reach for the slender straps of leather before he can jerk them back. When I grab the whip and pull it from him, Leon is caught off balance and nearly falls off his cart. For a moment, I see that he looks terrified.

Before either one of us can move, Angeline takes the reins and pulls the whip from me, flinging it out of the cart. She guides the sweating horses across the last cornfield into the barnyard and then unhitches them, leaving Leon and me in the cart. I'm breathing hard now, and I want to go further but I don't. I know that Leon is getting a whole lot more than he bargained for with me, though. Part of it is what I have stored inside me from years living with Joe, holding back. I've learned you can't knock a man who spends most of his time lying in his own piss and vomit. Leon is still standing, at least on the outside. But that night, I see that he is as scared as my dad. I remember what Red Otter said about the priest who beat the boys at the Indian school. *"You can fight back to defend yourself, Gilles, but when you fight any other way, you join them and they win. Remember, they win."* I hope for a middle road—something between killing them and killing myself, but I sure as hell haven't found it yet.

Leaving Home

Awakening at dawn, I slip away from the farm and crouch in the cornfield nearest the pull stop landing, waiting to hop an open freight car on the 11:27 Illinois Central from St. Louis. I've left a note in French for Ange, secured inside her buffalo bundle. I want her to know that it isn't her that I'm running from. I tell her that it is better having a Dad who is dead-drunk on Chicago streets than a living Leon. You might not always know where to find Joe, but at least there are no big surprises when you do.

Jumping into a freight car, I am soon lying on my back, rolling through midsummer cornfields, Chicago-bound, thinking about Leon. It is easier the farther away I get. At least I can breathe now. I tried being reasonable. I know there are a lot of reasons why Leon acts the way he does. I know that you don't get to be a man like him without a lot of bad things happening to you, both inside and out. I'm trying to understand, but I still can't figure it out.

I know if I stay in the colony, I will just get sicker. The anger in me will grow until it explodes. Then Red Otter will be proven right. I will have joined Leon and become just like him—hating others or, more likely, hating myself. You don't have to have blue eyes to be mean. Brown works fine.

Ange, I still can't figure. She and Leon have come a long way together. There is no mistaking her running down the ridge path to meet him the first day he arrived. That's real. Yet, I can see she pretends that he is something that he isn't, and most of the time, she ignores what he is. I also see that it was a lot harder for her to ignore this after I got there. It is strange, because I know Ange has clear vision about most things. She sees that I'm trying to save my father, even when I deny that I care. Also, she senses that, like Joe, I love the taste of smooth whiskey on my tongue. And it's clear to her that I'm looking for something I haven't found yet. The one thing I know is I don't want to leave her.

The train is late pulling into Chicago Central Station. We slow down in the stockyards. I try to sleep, but the hungry cattle are moaning; they aren't going quietly to their deaths. I jump off the train just before it enters the station, knowing that they check the cars for freeloaders. I'm excited now. Night is coming. . . . this is my time. I'm walking towards those Chicago dance halls, the Aragon, the Dreamland, the Savoy, where I'll catch the girls. I am at Dreamland's back door where I get a kiss from one of Joe's favorites and a couple of dollars. My lips on hers, I realize that it is a dark-eyed Métis I am looking for, and know that she wouldn't be dancing here, ever. The Dreamland bouncer recognizes me and lets me know that my dad has money tonight and has already been there, drinking.

My life. . . . I'm home.

Even though I bumped across Joe's path that first night, it takes me three days to find him. I've almost given up when I see him eating eggs at an all-night diner a block or two from the Savoy, where he appears to have spent most of the night, judging by the stack of empty glasses in front of him. Looking through the café glass, I watch him. A tall man, his muscled shoulders are hidden by a tailored coat. I notice a web of tiny red blood vessels spreading out across his nose, a spider web marking his dark skin, but I'm drawn to his eyes—a soft deep brown like Angeline's, Red Otter's, and mine—they are kind, gentle-looking. In the window, I slick back my hair and observe my own face. There is a connection between me and this man, and it is more than our similar appearances. I can't help thinking that I'm like Ange, blinded to some people, not seeing what is right in front of my face. When I walk in and sit down next to him, he is not surprised.

"Hello, Gilles. Eat up, I'm paying."

That's the kind of Dad he is. I am picked up by Social Welfare, disappear for half a year, walk in on him when he's eating breakfast, and he invites me to eat. No questions asked.

I do most of the talking. I tell him that I was taken to Southside Orphanage, and that they were gonna send me to one of those reservation schools, but instead I got "lucky" and was sent to the colony with Ange and Leon. He gives me no reaction until I mention Ange, and then he pulls that fancy liquor bottle out of his jacket pocket and pours it into his coffee, causing the milk to curdle across the top. He drinks it all.

Me, I don't eat. I just sit with him. Maybe I'm trying to test it out . . . is this really better than being with Leon? My stomach doesn't hurt; at least, not yet. With Leon, my stomach throbbed when I first saw him. With Joe, it comes on slow.

Two or three weeks later, I'm drinking harsh whiskey out of cheap bottles—no fine cut glass for me—and my stomach is aching. A Social Welfare lady who frequents the dance halls looking for delinquent kids had a couple policemen drag me from the Savoy back over to Southside. The fight in me is gone, I'm so ploughed. And so, here I am, stuck again in McDermott's office. He starts off by trying to convince me that the reservation schools are some sort of opportunity for a kid like me. I'm "eligible" for this special service. For hundreds of other kids, there is nothing but the Chicago streets.

"That's not nothing. The streets have everything." But after I say it to him, I feel my stomach rolling . . . am I gonna throw-up in his office? What is in this whiskey? I try to hide my gagging, but I know that he sees it.

"The only opportunity you've got is to become a drunk like your father. It doesn't matter then if you're whole-Indian, part-Indian, or no-Indian. Drunks are all the same, Gilles." His voice is so matter of fact. And I agree with him, but I'm not going to be like my Dad. McDermott doesn't need to worry there.

"So you think the way to fix me is a rez school, McDermott? My uncle was in one. That's when he started drinking. I can take care of myself," I spout.

"You can? You weren't drinking the last time I saw you." Still so rational, how does he manage to do it? Then again, this isn't his family. He should stick with them.

"No school is gonna stop this," I reply. "You wanna do something? Fix up that orphanage you got here. There's some kid up there who thinks he owns the place. He's taking a piece of all the kids who come through there. If you wanna do something, do that."

"Gilles, I'm trying here . . . but I also have got to do something with you. You're only fifteen—"

"—not old enough to be out on my own."

"Remember last time you were here? We talked about your dream to do something . . . change things for other kids."

"Well, I've changed. I just wanna take care of myself now, so forget that. You've got more than enough kids to take care of in this city. Do your job, take care of them. I don't need help."

McDermott stops talking, but I can see that he isn't going to give up on me. He mentions a job in a pawnshop. They want a kid who can speak a bunch of different languages. Meanwhile, I will have to stay in the orphanage. He'll put me on a different floor, but I know it's not over. McDermott won't be able to do anything about Jared. He writes down his name, but I know that nothing else will happen. After I leave his office, I stumble into the hallway and vomit into a trashcan. My head hurts like hell. He's right . . . I can't drink this stuff. It only takes a little bit and my head is swimming. It is the same with Dad; we are different from drunks who can handle bottles of the stuff.

❖❖❖

A week later I'm spending my days at a pawn shop, trying to convince Eddie, the owner, that I will be fine sleeping under the counter at night. He tells me that I don't know what I'm talking about—the store isn't safe for man or child, day or night. That's why he keeps a loaded gun under the counter. So I tell him about Jared and ask him how safe he thinks that orphanage is. He agrees. Eddie, an Irish man who has a well-honed ability to make friends with drunks, has more of a feeling about my safety than McDermott does.

"Nothing is safe, boy. You got that one right," he answers.

Eddie takes me on because he owes some favors to McDermott, who has helped him out years back by giving him a loan during a tough time. Eddie pays him back by taking on boys from "the home." He is a respectful kind of guy who gives his boys a pawned suit to wear and even tailors it down so that it fits right. "Carefully chosen attire is appreciated, Gilles, even in a pawn shop." Respectful as he is, he waits until my second week there to mention that he has known my Dad for years . . . Black Joe, he calls him. I don't ask how he knows him, but after that I'm always expecting to find one of Joe's suits in the boxes of old clothes that I help Eddie unpack and put on the shelves.

During my breaks, and sometimes even during slow periods, he lets me rifle through the boxes of books and read what I want. He is always telling me that reading is important—something he has always wanted to learn. He gets around his disability, as he calls it, by asking for a boy who "speaks languages," his code words for a boy who can read. During our breaks, I read to him—travel and adventure stories are his most frequent requests—but I also read him William Butler Yeats and George Bernard Shaw.

On one of these breaks, I see McDermott come through the front door of the shop for the first time. He has a visitor with him—a woman who wears a long, dark skirt of rough material topped by a white shirtwaist cinched with a woven belt of yellow and red. Her hair is coiled in a long braid that circles around her head. She has a wool shawl over her shoulders even though it is a hot day. I don't realize who she is until she is standing in front of me and I'm staring into her dark eyes.

"*Tawnshi kiya*, Gilles."

"Hello, Ange."

I have never been so glad to see anyone, and it's funny, I don't feel shocked. I'm not sure how I feel. It's not like I expected her but now that she's here I can see that we belong together. Just how did it happen? Why did she come? I find out that Red Otter died days after I ran away, begging Ange to find me. So she did.

Ange stays in Chicago for three months, before we ride the train to the colony. It is a long time—long enough for her to learn to swim at Michigan's pier (she and I wake up each morning and dive into the lake's icy waters before we work at Eddie's) and long enough for her to discuss my education with McDermott (he finds some Indian scholarship at the University of Chicago, but it is Ange who encourages him to investigate it after she discovers the University's library on one of her afternoon walks).

Her months in Chicago are not long enough to find Joe, however. Ange says she isn't looking for him, but I see her get up when the bars are closing and wander the streets. I'm sure he see us swimming in Michigan one morning. A dark figure on the shore raises his hand clutching a bottle—he raises his hand and waves. I don't tell her.

Our last night in Chicago I awaken to the explosive drumming of a summer thunderstorm. Our small room is suddenly fired with lightning and I see that Angeline is no longer asleep on her mattress. Where is she? I feel responsible. Chicago is my city, not hers. Even though I can see that she has become quite comfortable here during the last few months, I worry. People on the streets see an old Indian woman. She's strong but they don't know that. I pull myself out of bed and stumble through Eddie's pawn shop, tripping our piles of junk, and push open the front door. Immediately, I am blinded by a blast of warm rain blown in by the summer wind. I wipe my eyes and see her crouched on Eddie's front stoop, her head in her arms, her shoulders shaking. I touch her shoulder and she raises her face to me, her eyes swollen shut, a combination of tears and rain.

"I'm never going to find him, Gilles. Never see him again."

I don't need to ask who. At the time it occurs to me that she and I both want him so much. And it's not going to happen, for either one of us. No son for her. No Dad for me. I squat down beside her and put my arms around her, touching her wet skin. We sit like this for several minutes. When we go back inside, she huddles on Eddie's couch and I cover her with a blanket. I make her tea with some of the herbs she brought from the colony, wishing I could remember which ones cure heartache.

I try to talk. "Ange, it's not you. He just can't be there for others—not you, not me, no one. I'm his son, Ange, and I haven't seen him for months. It's nothing you did. Ange, please stop crying."

Finally she speaks, choking out the words, "I shouldn't have married Leon. Leon hated Joe, knowing he wasn't his son."

Although it is news to me, I'm not totally surprised about the Leon part. A braggart and a fake to most folks, but a real bastard to Joe, I bet.

"Ange, you're not Leon. You loved your son. It makes me sick to watch you walking the streets looking for him."

"Gilles, you didn't see how bad Leon treated him."

"Worse than me I guess . . . So, who is his dad?"

"Louie Riel, a leader of the Canadian government."

"Some leader. Where is the guy?"

"He was hung."

"Hung? My grandfather was hung! Why?"

"For leading a rebellion, or at least that's what others told me.

Gilles, he tried to save himself by pleading insanity, but they killed him anyway."

"Was he crazy, Ange?" A drunk father, a crazy grandfather. Figures. Lost in my own head, I am pulled back when I hear Ange sobbing loudly.

"Gilles, sometimes I think he was, but I loved him,"

Sitting on Eddie's stoop, I hold her until the rain stops and the sky fills with morning light.

That morning, I don't protest my return to the colony. Ange and I ride the train together guarding an over-stuffed satchel of books McDermott has given us.

Ange sleeps most of the trip back, but I enjoy sitting on the plush seats looking out the open windows, breathing in the near harvest corn— no freight car perfumed by animals for me this time. Just before we get to the colony, Ange wakes up and starts talking. "Gilles, I dreamt that you and I don't go back to living with Leon. Red Otter spoke to me and told me that we have to find another home."

I am not surprised by what she says. After all, she didn't mention Leon once during her stay in Chicago. "Where will we live, Ange?"

"Red Otter told me that we can live in his hut."

"That'd be just fine with me, Ange. I've got a lot of studying to do," I say, hoping that it will be.

Each of us leave that train for a new life—Ange has finally decided to leave Leon. And me, I am going to a "prep school" for the University of Chicago that is little more than a thatched hovel covered with bird's nests lying on a ridge above the Illinois River. Fine by me. I get my lectures from the crows.

Elisabeth – 1968

Chicago

Won't you please come to Chicago . . .
We can change the world.

—Graham Nash

The Ice

*F*rom Dad's rusted-out Plymouth station wagon I can see that the Illinois lake is peaceful, the gray sky backlit with wine-colored clouds from the late winter morning sun, the ice smooth, cleared of a light snow by an early March wind the night before. Each of us wants to be first on the ice. Grabbing our skates, we run, hoisting rubber duck boots in and out of heavy melting snow. My younger brother, Marc, who outstrips most of the school cross-country team, reaches the lake's edge first, but snaps a rotting string lacing his hockey skates. He loses out with a "Damn!" So Dad is the first to shove off, his ice hockey player's body slightly hunched over as he pumps hard to pick up speed. I skate after the disappearing dark figure, heading for the opposite shore. Beginning slowly, I pick up my pace, gaining on him until I reach the middle of the lake, throw my head back and spin in a circle. Eyes half-closed, long braid whirling, I nearly slam into Marc, who is skating close behind me.

"You think you're one of those acrobatic ice dancers, don't you?" His laugh echoes across the deserted lake, and then, surprising me, he reaches for my arm and twirls us around.

He is right. I often imagine I am an ice dancer. But this warm late-winter day, in the middle of the otherwise deserted frozen lake, I think instead that I am the only person left in the world—no popular high-school kids staring at me, no screaming children to baby-sit. For once I am free—looking up at my brother's grinning face—but obviously not alone. Our feet fall in line, and we skate parallel for several minutes. Marc hasn't guessed what I am thinking, but he knows enough to be quiet, so I dip into my other favorite winter fantasy. This time I am running behind my dog team, racing across Canada. My lead dog is driving hard. I am sweating. *Go . . . go.*

Marc's voice breaks into my tundra dream. "So where is he, Elisabeth?"

I look up. We are almost at the other side of the lake . . . no Dad. Usually the winner of our family race waits at the opposite shore.

"Don't know, Marc. There's not much wind today. He probably skated to the twin lake without us."

"Yeah, you did that last time, didn't you?"

A week ago, that time dreaming of ice caves, I left my father and brother and maneuvered along the narrow ice isthmus leading to another lake, a not-so-tame twin of this one. This sister lake is overgrown with tree roots, jagged granite rocks and jutting wedges of ice pushing up on its shore. Something about this lake captures me. It is private. I am alone. I know that my father likes it, too. Once I saw him there, skating powerfully, hips moving, arms stretched to the sky. He was dancing, surrounded by ice and sky, partnering with the wild one.

Marc and I set out for the narrow passage that joins the two sisters. I think I hear the first high-pitched crack as we glide onto the cape—a haunting *creeeaugh* followed by a gush, the noise of ice breaking. A second, sharper noise follows. I look at Marc. He has stopped skating. His eyes squint, straining to find our father. Nowhere. Then, around the turn on the other side of the isthmus, I see a human shadow on the ice. Dad's clear baritone voice shouts. Then he vanishes, leaving only a steel dark circle in the ice about twenty feet away. It is again quiet. I drop to my knees. Undaunted, Marc flies to the edge of the hole. I can see Dad's hat floating in the broken circle. I crawl, drenched in the frigid water thrown over the ice.

At the edge of the gaping pit, I cannot look up or down. Marc presses his face alongside mine, his crooked upper teeth clenched; he isn't talking, but I see points of light in his pupils, dark circles of fear.

His mouth is opening very slowly. "We have to do something." He is holding a long, curved stick. Where he got it, I have no idea, a remnant of a wild oak, maybe. Icy water laps at my ankles and quickly begins to fill my skates, but I'm not sinking. My mind is slowing down. . . . what is happening? Maybe the water is infusing it too.

"Elisabeth, take it."

Marc's voice is coming from miles away.

I reach up for the branch he offers. My gloves stick to the rough ice as I grip the edge. I hold on and force myself to look into the open cavity.

"Hold me," I say, ripping off my oversized army jacket.

Close to six feet tall at thirteen, Marc is already taller than most of the boys in my class. Kneeling at the edge of the icy water, he looks like a giant to me. I know when he grabs my ankles that he won't let me go.

Pushing off slowly from the sharp edge, I try not to think about Marc sliding into the watery pit with me. I guide my head down until I see a strange, blue light eerily filtering through the ice now above me. I feel the numbing water anesthetize the top of my head. Needle pricks, then nothing, all feeling gone. Drugged, I struggle to stay alert. Remember, I warn myself, breathe, breathe before you dive. I do and plunge my upper body in deeper, now no longer feeling my fingers . . . my arm fused to the branch. Am I still waving it? Is Dad here or has he fallen even further? I know this lake is a deep cavern. But how deep? With my legs held by Marc and my arms swimming in the ever-darkening water, first silver, now cobalt, my braid unraveling, I imagine myself an upside-down mermaid. The air space, a foot at most, is tough to find, but drawn by the ghostly blue candle-like glow, I rediscover it and gulp air, again and again. Breathing keeps my fear away. I tell myself that as long as I breathe, Dad is alive, too. I feel that I should be panicked, but I'm not, just stunned. I can't feel anything except my chest pushing in and out and my heart pounding.

Marc tells me later that Dad shot out of the water, but my swollen eyes are squeezed shut and I don't see anything. I only remember

Marc dragging me out, my fingers bleeding, cut by the jagged ice at
the edge of the void. Lying flat on the ice, I see them standing together.
They pull me up. Had I passed out? Dad is alive, shaking and talking
to me, "Save yourself." With this, he propels himself away and skates
toward the shoreline, long muscular movements easily visible under his
drenched flier's jacket and stinking woolen pants, his slicked-back black
hair already starting to freeze. What has he said . . . save yourself? Marc
waits until I am moving. His head is raised high. He is again scouting for
cracks. My legs, now tree stumps, shake. I skate close behind him until
we reach the opposite shore.

 I lay down in the heavy wet snow as soon as we reach the lake's
edge and feel my eyes close—*a little while, Marc, just let me sleep here*—
until his voice intrudes in my dream, commanding me, "Stay awake."

 I wake up in the back of our wagon, stripped naked but wrapped
in a worn army blanket. The car radio plays "Hey Jude." Marc and Dad
are singing along with it. I hear the wobbling hum of the car heater and
guess that Dad is cranking it to the highest temperature. A melting pile
of woolen winter clothing and sodden skates lie next to me. My eyelids
are heavy, I want to be back under the ice, see that ghost-like blue light
again.

 "Don't go to sleep on us, Elisabeth. We'll make you drive." Dad's
voice booms with laughter and hurts my ears. My head is throbbing,
fever-hot.

 "You look like a beet, sis." Marc smiles, but this time he isn't
laughing.

 I lie there, spread out in the back of the wagon, and want to
talk with them about what just happened, but my mouth won't work.
I have lost my words in that icy hole. For the first time I realize that
I am different from Dad and Marc. Until this moment, I have always
thought that we are exactly alike. We like to do the same things—hike the
Ridge Trail at the Grand Canyon, bodysurf the wild Wolf River Falls in
Wisconsin, and skate on lakes that lack not only lights and hot chocolate

stands, but people. We are competitive, not so much with others, but among ourselves. One of us is always going to the far side, the others racing to follow. At the same time I always know, just as I had when Marc lowered me under the ice, that neither he nor Dad would let me fall. And neither Marc nor I would have left Dad in that silver wasteland. Yet, I am starting to understand how we are different. The physical stuff, that's easy. I have to work harder to keep up with them. I still win some of our races, but not as many. But today, I realize something else. There isn't any way that I am going to sing along with that car radio after going under the ice. I have to believe that they are feeling some of what I am. I'm convinced that Dad, Marc, and I have been given a second chance today. I have never been persuaded by the dogma-loving Catholicism that my mother espouses, promising salvation, but this is different. I am thoroughly convinced by this experience that there is a purpose for our rescue, and I want to talk about it.

Half an hour later, the three of us are sitting in Paul's Place, a highway truck stop a few miles from our house, waiting for Dad's favorite—chili dogs with extra onions. We made a five-minute pit stop at home to change clothes, or, in my case, to put on clothes. Standing in front of my bedroom mirror, I wonder just how they managed to pull them off me on the shore of that lake. Had they seen me naked? Of course I can see it was a practical matter. Leaving any of us in frigid clothing would have led to hypothermia. I already stopped shivering; maybe I would have slept forever. But I wonder what their thoughts were when they pulled off my army surplus parka, jeans, wool stockings, silk long underwear. Would they notice that? What else had they noticed? My skin is still red, more the color of salmon than beets now, and my legs and arms tingle as they come back to life. My dripping hair brings back my mermaid fantasy; and I relive myself extended in that icy world. I imagine how my father looked, his arms and legs moving powerfully under the water, searching for the hole, each of us breathing again and again. I did not see him, but we were there together.

Standing in front of the jukebox at Paul's, Dad pops in a quarter and says that he saw me, first a movement . . . my stick, then a ripple of blue, probably my sweater, finally my hair. I am amazed that he thinks he saw my hair. Why do I care about how he escaped? What mattered was that he saw something, anything, found the hole, propelled himself out of the water and skated out of that cracking winter paradise. I want to ask him if he really said, "Save yourself." It doesn't fit with the way I see him. Wouldn't he have stayed to help Marc and me, or at least have waited until we were ready to go with him? But he didn't. I know that he believes in the two of us. Maybe he knew that we were going to make it to the opposite shore, even when we didn't. His faith galvanized us.

I realize standing with him there that I'm still not sure that we *have* made it. I try to repeat what he said. *Save yourself.* I manage to mumble the words in spite of my chattering teeth, but I still don't believe that he said them.

The Physical Stuff

*A*s a Chicago high school student, when I'm not dreaming about being an ice dancer, sled driver, or mermaid, I am thinking about sex. During my junior and senior years I go to school half-time and work twenty hours a week as a butcher's assistant at Jewel Food Store. This plan is supported by my father, who believes that all teens should have jobs as insurance against catastrophe. On weekends, I usually swim, bike, or hike another 6 or 7 hours with my dad and brother, for a total of 47 hours a week, approximately equal to the time that I spend sleeping—100 hours of productive activity each week allowing me close to 70 to dream about sex. This is not to say that I'm not fantasizing about sex when I'm sitting in Mr. Marcone's physics class or slicing pounds of chemically-dyed pink ham at Jewel. If anything, activity fuels my imagination, especially repetitious mind-numbing activity, of which there is an overwhelming amount in my high school. Hortense Dalton, an English teacher with 35 years experience, articulates what the other teachers are thinking but are too cool to say—"Keep them busy so that they won't have time to think about it." That is her classroom mantra, chanted by her former students, so she keeps us occupied looking up endless lists of words in Webster's with no apparent order other than alphabetical, and often not even that. We copy selected prose and poetry written in the 19th century. Anything from the 20th century might incite passion, and pre-birth control Midwestern America shies away from promoting or even acknowledging teenage desire. However, the way I see it, the more Miss Dalton (or Hortense, as we frequently call her behind her back) and the other teachers try to prevent us from paying attention to our newly developed and easily stimulated bodies, the more they fail.

Hortense believes that the Good Humor ice cream truck that visits our school parking lot on warm, humid spring days is dispensing rubbers and LSD, along with Eskimo Pies, creamsickles, and orange popsicles. She reported the driver to our school principal, who believed her. He then invoked a city ordinance that forbade commerce on high school grounds. Now the kindly Czech-speaking Good Humor man, who has never understood Hortense's complaints about him, has to be satisfied with visiting the elementary and middle schools. Surely, no condoms or drugs will be purchased with grade-schoolers' sticky nickels and dimes. Although I trust Hortense Dalton's detective skills, I've never purchased anything from the Good Humor man, neither rubbers nor ice cream. Miss Dalton has a lot more time to waste than I do, and she is clearly not as focused on her sexual life. Initially, I appreciate her involvement in the lives of her students. She tells us that she and several other teachers pray for our souls on a daily basis and invites us to join her Bible study group at a local Christian college, a force that already exerts undue influence on our public high school. She emphasizes the fact that sex equals sin in God's eyes, and her definition of what constitutes sex includes anything that a teenager might even think about doing.

On a warm late spring afternoon that would benefit from the missing and now demonized ice cream man, I am sitting in the back of her class, staring at the parking lot where the truck once rested. Hortense is in the front of the class praying for our souls, when her wobbly but surprisingly sweet chant takes an unexpected turn. She begins walking across the front row, then stops to pray at the desk of my closest friend, Marlene, who is sitting in the second row. I see Marlene quickly cover her pink cheeks with her hands. On her left ring finger she wears the gilded gold class ring of the senior class president. The room is suddenly very quiet, Hortense's voice a whisper. I strain to listen but can't hear anything until Marlene's disgraced cry fills our classroom. Hortense has been praying for mothers everywhere until she directs her prayer at the hidden mother-to-be who sits in the first desk of the second row. Hortense knows. Marlene's scream flows into the bell that announces the end of class, and mercifully the other students flee. Marlene slides from her chair and drops to her knees at the front of the evacuated classroom. Her hunched shoulders are heaving, the missing father's varsity letter sweater protectively caressing them. She doesn't move when I first touch her arm. Minutes pass . . . finally I link my hand in hers and pull her up. Hortense is watching us, her lips still moving, praying. She does nothing while I guide Marlene out of the classroom and through the back door of the school; hand-in-hand we walk to the gravel parking lot. We sit on the curb in our high socks and penny loafers, dragging our feet in the pebbles where the Good Humor man used to park, until Marlene's partner in sin drives his father's Chevy over to pick us up.

Marlene never comes back to high school after that afternoon, and I transfer out of Hortense's class, terrified that one day she will stop at my desk and pray for me. She ignores me until I'm chosen for the role of a teasing prostitute in a junior class play based on Edgar Lee Master's "Spoon River Anthology." I don't want this part in the beginning, but a supportive and provocative drama teacher who does not yet fully understand the religious underpinnings of our high school convinces me to try it. Although initially put off, I come to love the role. I think of Marlene, now living in a home for unwed mothers in St. Louis, and articulate my lines with a courage that I cannot show in my real life.

No sooner are my first lines out of my mouth at the initial rehearsal than Hortense is again praying for my soul and now advocating my early release from high school. Hortense's detective skills are first rate. She hears about my part, in her words that of a "fallen woman," and attends a rehearsal where she is thoroughly offended. Then she hisses her message to students, teachers, and even more importantly, the principal, who is afraid of her ability to mobilize the "Christian" community against him. "The girl was Marlene's best friend. This choice of part is no accident. It reflects her character." The drama teacher, who hasn't heard about what happened to Marlene, stands up for his play and for me, but Hortense is insistent. Finally, a compromise is made. The play can be performed at theatrical competitions, but never at our high school. I will have my part and be able to speak for the girls who are sexual, just never at my home. I settle for it. I have no choice. I have seen what Hortense's prayer can do.

Our play does well in competition, eventually winning second place in the state finals. I return home from the performance unable to stop playing my part. I practice it while I apply eyeliner in front of the cracked bathroom mirrors, mumble it walking between classes, and one day, alone in the school auditorium, I pop on the theatre lights and shout it from front center stage, embellishing it with several four letter words. An unseen audience claps for several seconds. Blinded by the footlights and feeling exposed, I shout, "Who are you?" Robert Anaquad, a junior who works on the lighting crew, runs up the aisle of the theatre and bumps into Hortense, who is standing at the auditorium door, and knocks them both to the ground. While they are lying stunned on the floor, I try to take stock of the situation. I'm not sure how much of this performance she has heard, but wanting to shock her, I hope that she was there for most of it.

Robert Anaquad's presence and admiration leaves me with an entirely different feeling. I want to sink into the stage floor with embarrassment. He has probably been here for all of it. I'm trying to remember what I know about him . . . I have seen him smoking in the back of the bus with the rest of the stage crew. I flash on a memory of his shoulder-length dark hair shooting across a muscled shoulder as he adjusts the footlights. I also remember that once, when Dad and I were swimming together, he mentioned this kid—a full blood Sioux, just off the reservation, and asked me if I could make him welcome at school. This was a curious comment coming from Dad, who shies away from any reminder of our mixed blood. Hortense doesn't give me much time to think.

"Just what are you two doing in here?" she shouts, interrupting my thoughts.

"What are *we* doing? What are you *thinking*?" I answer her, but just a little too fast. I have time to see the sharp pain in Anaquad's eyes before he shields them with his hair. The word that I had used—*we*—an impossible insinuation that he and I could be a we, he heard, too. And he clapped for me. Good detective that she is, Hortense also catches my meaning.

"Well, if nothing was going on, is there another problem here?" she returns.

His voice is barely audible. "No problem, Miss Dalton, I was working the lights, and I stopped to listen to her talk."

A glint of new understanding flashes in Hortense's faded eyes. Smiling, she moves in for the attack again. "Just what was she saying, Robert?"

His long hair is completely covering his face now, but his voice is clear, "Just what you say, Miss Dalton."

"What I say, Robert?" Hortense is curious now.

"Yes . . . the Our Father, prayers and stuff."

"She was praying on stage?" This shocks her and surprises me. A quick, well-armed defense.

"Yeah."

"And you clapped because she was praying on stage?"

"She prays real well."

Only inches apart, Hortense's anger warms the air connecting the three of us. I can feel their breathing, his low and even, hers a rapid pant. I get the sense that she is a little embarrassed, but not nearly as embarrassed as we are. I'm only too glad when she insists that the three of us leave the auditorium immediately. We do. Anaquad runs across the parking lot, and confirming my suspicion that she feels guilty,

Hortense asks me if I want a ride home. I don't take it.

That night, lying in bed, I replay everything. I see Anaquad's brown cheeks tighten and fade from copper to a ghost-like gray before he shields them with a dark curtain of hair, still uncommon at my high school. His left arm, the one that he accidentally knocked Hortense over with, can't stop shaking. I sense both desire and fear when his eyes lock into mine.

The next day at school, I spread the word that I am looking for him. With hundreds of students, gossip is the only way to find anyone. My girlfriends are curious. Why am I interested in him? But they agree to help me out—after all, I have acted strange since Marlene's last day. I don't ask them what they think of him. At this point I really don't care. After several days pass and there's still no sign of him, I give up on the school grapevine and search the campus—backstage, the football field, baseball lots, corridors of rusted-out lockers and even the boys' bathrooms—nothing. Our mutual acquaintances tell me that Anaquad has "family business" and that I'm not going to be able to locate him. Two days later, he finds me—working the late shift at Jewel Food Store.

I have just finished cleaning the meat slicer and am hooking the curved blade back into place when I see his face reflected in the glass case in front of the delicatessen. His hair is slicked back from his forehead, revealing the intense eyes that were hidden from me in the auditorium. No embarrassment visible now—these eyes say "I dare you," and his voice is confident when he asks if I need a ride home at the end of my shift. I already have a ride: my father, who shows up before I can answer Anaquad's question. He takes a long look at our faces, nods at Anaquad, takes the waiting reduced-price meat that I'm allotted by my job, and tells me to be home by one in the morning.

Anaquad rode to Jewel on his motorcycle, a 450 Harley that knows the back roads. With us on it, the Harley spins out of the Jewel lot, spraying the parked cars with a fine gravel rain before it heads into a narrow two-lane highway, Butterfield Road, the sole remnant of the old pioneer trail that zigzagged across northern Illinois. It is a warm night with enough of a moon that I can see single leaves hanging on the oaks lining the road and count individual dark hairs on the back of Anaquad's neck. I'm not exactly a novice. I have taken rides with boys on motorcycles, but I feel different with him. Anaquad and his Harley operate as one. His shoulders press hard into the wind as we start pulling up Blackhawk hill north of Naperville. His denim shirt blows out behind him, pressing against me, and his back muscles are tense, glowing in the moonlight. Going downhill I feel his body relax under mine. I sit upright, pull back on the worn leather seat, embarrassed by the flimsy yellow rayon dress that the butchers have chosen for their two female apprentices. My gauze uniform is both feel-through and see-through, selected so that the butchers can watch our anatomy enter the meat freezer. With my body close to his, I stiffen—holding back so that he won't feel my nipples tighten against his back, trying not to feel the curves of his stomach enclosed in my sweaty palms. After Naperville, we reach the end of the farmlands and move into open fields. His shoulders press back into my chest, and finally, I relax and lay my head on his back, resting my face against his hair. We are crossing a newly planted cornfield of young seedlings. The spring sky lights up more stars with each moment and becomes a dark blanket wrapping up the two of us.

Unlike the other boys I've ridden with, Anaquad doesn't speed. He's going for the ride—long, even, and steady—and he wants me to relax and enjoy it. He doesn't stop until we are a block away from my house, when he kills the motor, pulls over and asks why I have been looking for him. My arms are still around his stomach, my head presses into his back. Neither of us move while I try to think of a good answer. I was looking for him so I should probably apologize for my stupidity in not seeing what is now pretty obvious to me. But I have no idea how to tell him that Hortense was a better detective than I. When I don't answer him, Anaquad turns his neck and moves his lips softly into the top of my head. I want to find his mouth and return the kiss, but at the same time,

I don't want to let go of him. His hands are free, though, and he searches for mine, loosening my lock-hold around his stomach and moving them higher so that they touch his hardened nipples. I feel the small fine hairs that encircle them and he begins to rock against me with the growing force of his muscles underneath. He arches back, pressing hard against my chest, and then I hear him moan. I struggle to answer him but my own new sounds are getting lost on their way out. His body is thrusting hard against mine now, and surprising myself, I push back against him and move my fingers underneath his shirt to his chest. Touching his nipples gives me a stunning power. My hips push forward on the seat until it feels like our lower bodies are joined. His face is turned away from mine so I can't see his eyes when his whole body spasms and he lets out a long, low scream. After this he turns his whole body around and pulls me onto his lap. I am afraid to look at him, not wanting him to see how aroused I am. Closing my eyes doesn't protect me here, though. He knows that I'm excited. He strokes my back, his pulsing lap forcing my body to join his rhythm. Eyes half shut, I see it all, his brown lips seeking my tongue and sucking it into his mouth, our jerky hip movements together, the wet stain on his Levis, and finally the red flush that spreads down my neck, covering the upper part of my body, all without a word spoken. Fantasizing about sex is one thing, this ride with him something entirely different. After this he drives quietly up the rest of the street and kisses me for several minutes outside my house. I don't go in after he rides away, but lie down in the grass covered by our sky blanket of night stars and listen to the steady hum of his motorcycle on Butterfield Road.

Going Steady

*D*ad and Marc have already left for the lake by the time I awake at 11 the morning after the motorcycle ride. Still savoring my last dream of Anaquad, I walk downstairs barefoot and quietly for me. I do not want to see my mother. No luck. She is hunched over the kitchen table, her lined face framed by a bouffant halo of silver-blonde hair, and she is focused on writing her grocery list. "Good morning," I say. No response. I sit down and pour my own coffee. She is sitting so close to me that her elbow knocks against my arm each time she comes to the end of a row, organized by the items needed for an individual dish—*potatoes, onions, cheese, chicken, garlic, black olives, red wine* . . . and with this she bumps my coffee cup, splashing my hand. I lick the milky brown liquid off my fingers and reach across for the cracked pot resting on the table. Out sputters a few drops.

"There is no more coffee." She speaks in a clipped voice continuing her list . . . *baby lettuce.* . . .

"I'll make more," I say as I caution myself—*Don't get into it with her, she wants to fight with you.*

"The kitchen is closed."

"When did it close?"

"When you came late to breakfast."

There can be no argument here. She is the kitchen. If she says it is no longer open, well, that's the way it is.

"I'll go out to breakfast then." By now I am angry, and struggle to keep my voice calm.

"Will you be riding a motorcycle?' Her clipped voice drops into anger when she asks this, but her lips are sealed in a tight smile, her pale gray eyes focused on the lined paper. But I sense her overture before it comes. "I will put coffee on the list."

"At the end," I say.

"Yes, at the end."

Whenever it's for me, it's always at the end. Mom sure values her rules more than me. I get up to leave, carrying my empty cup to the sink to wash. I don't need breakfast. In fact, I don't want breakfast in a kitchen where disapproval is the first item on the list. Hungry, I grab a ripening pear off the windowsill.

"Just where are you going?"

"The kitchen is 'closed.' I'm leaving."

"You will get in deep trouble with that boy."

She is no longer working on her list, and I see that this is the breakfast menu today . . . a lecture I do not want to hear. I don't want to fight with her, but don't see how to avoid it. Her anger is palpable. It reaches across the kitchen table and wraps me in a vise. I warn myself, *Don't snap back.* In a controlled voice, I ask, "Oh, really? How does that happen?"

"*Quand j'étais jeune, tous les garçons. . . .*" *When I was young, all the boys. . . .*

She has switched to French now, her voice moving a fraction higher with each word. In French, she has the advantage—speed. I lean against the hard-edged formica and steel myself for her speech, which breaks into a prayer, "*Poor little child, may a merciful God help you,*" for Marlene's baby due this week. Feeling the sharp edge of the counter against my back, I notice that if I stare straight at my mother's face, I can ignore what she is saying. Almost. My mother's eyes are luminous; a radiant gray that can be soothing. However, this morning they are steel searchlights. Although I am trying hard not to listen, I catch just enough of her words . . . *Dieu*, rumination, *Dieu*, careless, *Dieu*, unloving. Shades of Hortense.

"I am not unloving." Damn. Now she knows I'm listening.

She does not hide her satisfied smile. "No, you're not unloving, but you were not paying attention to me, and you will end up in trouble."

Although my mother doesn't know it, I already feel like I'm "in trouble," not because I'm in imminent danger of being sent to St. Madeline's Home for Unwed Teenage Mothers, but because I'm falling in love with Anaquad. My nighttime dream of his swollen brown lips, hard back, and dark-shadowed eyes will claim my days. No place will be safe from this vision of him. As we speak, my gray-eyed, silver-haired mother is being transformed into a six-foot male with straight brown-black hair. As he reaches out to pull me closer, I hear my mother's sharp voice rise to a screech, and it breaks my trance. What is she saying? I have no idea because I'm back on the Harley, no longer holding my body stiffly but pressing my nipples up against Anaquad's chest, relaxing my arms against his body. I drop the pear and escape from the kitchen, but I'm not left alone.

These fantasies soon intercept everything—my job at Jewel, Marcone's Physics class. No place offers sanctuary. He is suddenly everywhere. I drift from school to home to job, my body captured by his spirit. Most days, I relive fantasies of the nights I have imagined, and I ride that motorcycle across Butterfield Road four or five times a day.

But the real nights are going to change, too. Anaquad and I are going to do a whole lot more than ride motorcycles. One late summer afternoon he and I rediscover Herrick's Lake, the scene of my father's near drowning. He picks me up after I work a long afternoon slicing hams at Jewel. We ride to the lake on his motorcycle, a journey just long enough to get me aroused, initiating a body flush that I have now learned reveals my growing excitement.

Anaquad notices it first. "What is this?" he poses as he lightly presses his index finger on the reddened skin just below my collar bone. Both his question and his touch spark a companion flush across my face.

I'm not sure what it is but I'm guessing it has a lot do with my feelings for him.

For Anaquad it is a similar story—for him it is an expanding wet stain on his Levi's, signaling that we are moving a bit too fast. I want to touch it, in the same way that he pressed his finger on me, but instead I only point. He looks down and turns away quickly, laughing when he hears my whispered answer, "I'll tell you if you tell me." He avoids responding by turning and running directly into the lake, plunging into the cool dark water, still fully clothed. I stand on the shore laughing and shout, "Now you're all wet, Anaquad."

"Come in, Elisabeth. . . ." I can see him jerking his clothing off under the water. He throws it toward me, and I run in, too, nearly getting hit by one of his shoes. Grabbing me, he helps me pull off my own soaking jeans and clinging gauze shirt, then holds my body tightly to his. Pushing me away suddenly, he climbs up onto the shore rocks overhanging this side of the lake and dives deep into the black water, swimming underwater until he glides next to me. Swooping me into his arms, he pulls me back into his stomach and cradles my body against his as we float together. Eventually, we get out and lie under the curved oak trees that line the shore, searching out the grassy parts to avoid tattooing ourselves with glacier-pebbles.

Lying on the bank that night, I discover that Anaquad can climax without any assistance from me, but that he isn't going to turn down an offer of help. So, my exploration of his body starts. Again and again, I seek the power that touching him brings me. His fingers, belly, and ass respond to even a light brush of my fingers, and when I stroke his cock, his face hardens and contorts, and his frame convulses as he groans with pleasure. His brown lips hide a mouth and tongue that explores my entire body. Now out of the lake, he laps the water from my arms and legs. Once we are dry by the night air, he searches out the still-moist crevices—under my arms, between my toes, inside my legs—and makes them as wet as the lake had.

I want to suck his body as freely as he mine, but find myself struggling, especially with his penis. The girls who "give head" at my school rapidly lose their popular status. I'm not exactly popular, but I'm not a pariah. "I'm not a slut," I whisper to him.

"I see what you're worried about," he responds, "but it's the opposite of the way that I see it, Elisabeth."

"But if someone else finds out?"

"Who's gonna tell?"

When I ask again, greatly fearing the sluttish reputation that quickly surrounds girls known to be adept with their mouths, Anaquad reminds me that he is only a junior and a marginally popular kid—who would believe him if he did tell? I don't think he will, but I need to hear him say it. It hurts me to hear him describe himself that way, to be reminded of that day in the auditorium when Hortense confronted me and I denied a possibility of anything between us.

As the summer moons come and go, I begin my own exploration, spurred on by his enthusiasm for everything I try. This is the beginning of the summer of '68. I, a member of the class of '69, understand the sexual gymnastics associated with my year's number, a huge point in my high school class. But this isn't the way it truly works with my class; despite lost popularity, the girls are usually giving head and the boys receiving it. But not so with Anaquad. I feel lucky, but also awkward. He is the expert here. Eventually, it dawns on me that I'm just plain afraid of his penis. It isn't the pregnancy factor but something even more primitive.

First, I don't have one, so my familiarity quotient is low. Next, he seems overly familiar with it. It is like a third partner on our dates, his partner more than mine. And last, I worry that I will bite or suck on it in a way that will cause him unbelievable pain. When we are lying in the grass, his cock in my mouth, I wonder if I will hurt him? And more, will he hurt me?

Chicago

*T*he summer of 1968 is hot, humid, and marked with a kaleidoscope of electric storms. Lying on the hood of the Plymouth at Herrick's Lake, Anaquad and I count the jagged streaks of lightning as they strike the lake. One night, we watch a giant red pine on the edge of the steepest granite glacier bluff join with the sky's fire, ignite, and topple into the murky green water below. The electric storms light our naked bodies. We are not afraid, at least not of lightning.

From numerous hours spent lying in the sun with him, reading teenage girl magazines and applying suntan oil, I turn dark.

"Brune brûlée," my mother calls me. "You have ruined your sensitive skin, *ma chère.*"

I feel "burned brown" when I hold my arm next to her ivory-colored one, bleached daily with a homemade lemon-rosewater lotion. What she doesn't say and I hear anyway, is *"Let it fade, you'll look less Indian."* While my skin darkens, my brown hair goes another way and, by August, it is shot through with red and white gold streaks, aided by hidden sprays of "Summer Blond." It looks like it was struck by the night lightning. Unlike mine, Anaquad's skin and hair move together in the same dark direction, deepening in color and intensity.

"White girl, brown boy." We hear it more than once that summer. First in an inquisitive way from my assistant manager at Jewel, who my co-workers tell me passed his time watching Anaquad and I neck in the Jewel parking lot.

"Just exactly what is he? Do you know anything about his family?" the store manager asks.

White girl, brown boy.

It doesn't fit with the way I feel when he and I are together. More and more, I'm starting to feel my Indian blood. Before Anaquad, I worried about my Indian blood, secretly believing that it is the reason I am not more popular. It isn't that I want to hang out with the popular kids, I don't. But I want to be wanted by them. The kids that I work with at Jewel are far better companions, working towards college and often helping to support their families while they are in high school. But it sure seems like the popular ones know how to party and have fun.

I also start paying attention to different things my parents say. After the near-drowning at Herrick's Lake, Dad starts talking some about Angeline, comparing me to her. Beginning when we are snowshoeing. "You've powerful legs, graceful like her." And swimming. "You've got it—her coordinated stroke." His words help me feel better about myself. I know that I don't look like my mother, whose petite, shapely, blonde French beauty evokes more street admiration than my muscular, athletic frame ever will. I also realize that I don't look like Dad, whose tan skin and straight black hair attract querying looks and sometimes disparaging comments even in his well-chosen business suits for his work as an attorney. I'm a mix. But what is that? The people I see handle it differently. I know that Mom is Métis, part Cree too, but I can see that she is trying hard to make her Indian part as small as possible. I guess that she is using a hair dye stronger than the temporary rinse that I spray on. Dad's Indian part looks stronger, at least from the outside, but then he hasn't talked about it with me a lot, at least not until recently. That summer, we drive to the Métis colony in western Illinois where he was raised by Angeline for the funeral of his aunt, Madeline Junot. I am watching him, and then, *Alloii* . . . the death chant starts and Dad begins to cry. No sound with the tears other than his baritone voice merging with the others. It is here that I become aware that Dad knows all the chants—English, French, and that funny language he calls Prairie Tongue, the words of the Métis—and Mom doesn't. He spoke English with a strange accent he struggled to hide until he took a course at the local college when I was in junior high.

Sometimes I believe that my confusion about who I am reflects their confusion. Do they feel they had to choose, too? But then, how confused am I? Other times I relate my mystification to loyalty struggles when I see Mom as French and Dad as Indian. But that doesn't work either. It simplifies something that isn't easy.

Being with Anaquad calms me. I feel I can talk to him about everything—French, Indian, Mom, Dad . . . anything. Even though we look different, I feel we are the same. But even so, things are changing.

Our sexual lives are really changing. Now, we lie next to each other without touching by mutual agreement—a period of temporary chastity—in order to take the time to learn more about each other, mostly his idea. We also talk nonstop. I reveal my struggles with my mother. Why is she so Catholic and, even more important, why does she expect me to believe what the bishops tell her? Don't I have a choice in what I think? Maybe it isn't the sex part that she hates, but the fact that Anaquad is Indian. Sometimes, I talk about my dad. I hope that he approves of my relationship with Anaquad, even though he only mentioned it once, when he asks me if I am being safe. He never said what he meant by safe. If he meant no-baby-safe, I am fine there. If he meant guarding-my-heart-safe, I am not fine, not fine at all. I do not feel safe. No, it isn't lightning I worry about, but a lot of other things. Ever since my dad's near drowning, I am scared that he will die . . . a car crash, a heart attack, even another drowning. . . . He will die, and I will be left with my mother. I will be forced to become a devout Catholic, maybe even give up sex forever and become a nun. Mom will want that, and I will resign myself to it. Maybe that's why I am starting to hold back now. Anaquad gently jokes with me about my fears, telling me that he is sure I will make a loyal nun, but he knows that I can never be celibate. He promises to visit me in the convent. Some days the convent sounds less risky than being in love with Anaquad.

Anaquad's newfound asceticism is also associated with a growing passion for politics—Indian politics. He tells me about some of the leaders he has met, young leaders, names I have heard from my dad who does some tribal pro-bono work—Russell Means, Clyde Bellecourt. Anaquad says they are going to bring power back to the tribes. The old leaders are useless. They lost everything. I listen, but don't feel like I can speak. I'm not sure what has been lost. Anaquad describes the Sioux reservation where he spent his childhood with his parents and sister. Like a lot of Indian families moving to Midwestern cities, they came to Chicago to find work and off-reservation schools for their kids.

Finally, late one night after the sky's psychedelic lightning show at Herrick's Lake, Anaquad talks about his family. Every time I asked before, he refused. "Don't, Elisabeth." Now I learn why.

At night, he tells me, his father drinks bottles of home-brewed beer made in a backyard still. Usually he sleeps outside, next to his empties. Some nights he stumbles inside, each time ripping his knuckles on the ragged screen door that blocks his path. Seeing his hand cut, he rages at his son and wife, smacking their bodies with his bleeding fist.

That night, Anaquad tells me that he just punched his father for the first time. "Self-defense, Elisabeth. That man thinks he can pound me? I'm not gonna take that shit." The next night at the lake, he discloses that it was "more than a hit." "I was on top of him, and I started belting him until he puked up all that beer. I guess I wanted to pound it out of him. But I couldn't stop myself. And I didn't want to." At the end of it, his father lay in a crumpled pile on the kitchen linoleum. From far way, he heard his sister's voice. "Anaquad . . . you'll kill him! Don't! He's our father." Lying in my arms, Anaquad tells me that if she hadn't called to him, he knew what he would have done—slain his father.

This year we are both learning that fathers can die. My father's father, Joe—a guy I'd never met, died in the early spring of liver cancer, an old man. Not too hard to understand that. Old people do die. And Dad told me enough to let me know that my grandfather drank to the point where he no longer cared about himself or those around him. Then, in April, Martin Luther King Jr. is shot and killed. In June, Robert Kennedy. So he and I are also learning that not-so-old men die. And that summer, we discover that teenagers like us die, too.

In August, the month of shooting stars, four months after we start dating, the Democratic convention is held in Chicago. Anaquad wants to go. He tells me kids will be coming from all over . . . young people, like us, who want to change things . . . not like the students in our high school. These kids want to change the world, and they know that not just men but boys are dying—by the thousands. The Tet Offensive in Vietnam is mounted that spring. And it is brought home by television news: spinning helicopters, exploding bombs, burning jungles, and contorted Asian faces sharing their final grimaces with us, their enemies, thousands of miles away while we calmly eat our dinners. I listen to Anaquad carefully, feeling like I still belong in the group of kids who only want sex. He puts me with those who want to change things. I ask him what I have ever tried to change. He reminds me that I spoke out for free speech in our high school when "Spoon River" was censored. I listen to him, but am not convinced. Wanting to speak my part as it was written for our high school play and going to a rally in Chicago to change the world are not exactly the same thing. Anaquad tells me that he is going to this convention, even if I'm not. And, although he doesn't say it, I can tell that he feels like I'm letting him down.

The morning before the Democratic convention begins, Anaquad and I are hanging out in the Jewel parking lot and hear our favorite disc jockey at WLS announce that a seventeen-year-old Sioux Indian from South Dakota, Dean Johnson, has been shot by the Chicago police. The police say that he pulled a gun. Though our transistor radio is loaded with static, the message finally comes through—the kid is dead. Anaquad starts shaking and talking about needing to do something. His left arm, the one that can not stop spasming when he is anxious, is trembling. He and two of his friends decide to drive to Chicago right away. I stay home, waiting by the telephone. An hour later, Anaquad calls and tells me that he and his friends are on Wells Street standing guard with another young Sioux at the spot where Dean Johnson was shot.

He tries to get me to go again. "Shit, Elisabeth, your Dad is Indian, you need to be here, tonight. There is going to be a march—a memorial—don't you want to be part of this?" I don't. I'm scared, but I don't want to tell him that. I hang up the phone and keep listening to the radio. Let him think whatever he wants. My teen station is now running hourly updates on the Chicago scene.

By now, Democrats, demonstrations, and teenagers are converging on Chicago. Mayor Richard Daley is threatening to bring in the National Guard, thousands of troops. That afternoon I take my transistor to Jewel Foods, playing it low in the back of the deli while I slice the dyed sandwich meat, folding it in neat packages. But I can't stop thinking about Anaquad. I decide to leave my afternoon shift early, get in my car and drive, still listening to my transistor and wishing I had a car radio, finally I end up at the Northwestern Train Station. The 6:03 Express is on time, just 41 minutes out of Chicago's loop, and Dad is on it. He doesn't act surprised that I am there to pick him up.

He gets in the passenger side and rolls down the car window. "So, where are we going?"

The radio is louder now as the Mayor's voice announces that 6,000 National Guardsmen have been mobilized and are practicing riot-control maneuvers.

He nods at the radio propped on the dashboard and asks, "Is that where we're going?"

I shrug, but start driving toward Pearl Road, the fastest link to the expressway. Funny, I knew he would go with me, but I didn't know how to ask him.

"They're checking ID's, Elisabeth."

"I have my driver's license."

"That may not be enough. What's up?"

Now it is my time to nod at the radio, and say, "There's going to be a riot."

"That's what I think, too. So tell me why we're in a car driving there?" He knows. I know. But he is going to make me tell him.

"Anaquad and his friends are having a vigil at the spot where the police killed Dean Johnson." I know I won't have to explain to him who Dean Johnson is. That he will know. I add to myself . . . *Dad wouldn't have done anything, but he would know, at least.* Maybe I am too hard on him? What can be done? He is coming with me, almost no questions asked. I watch him open a Chicago street map that he keeps in the glove compartment.

"Do you know if Anaquad was there when they shot him, Elisabeth?"

"He wasn't. He and his friends went over there later, they're keeping some sort of honor guard."

His eyes narrow; he seems to be counting things. "How long ago did you talk to him?"

"Three hours, maybe."

"Well, if we're lucky, he's not in jail yet, but I wouldn't count on it."

We drive silently, listening to a replayed description of Dean's shooting, and the evolving plans for the police . . . riot gear, tear gas, bayonets, billyclubs. . . .

Looking over at my Dad, I can see that he is tired. He has taken off his sunglasses and is rubbing his eyes. "Have you called Anaquad's parents? And your mom?"

"No, I didn't think of it."

"We can do it from my office."

"I want to drive to Wells Street."

"We can try, but I don't think we're going to be able to. They were already checking ID's outside my building, and that's blocks away."

"So, what can we do at your office?" Now that I finally have the courage to go, I'm not going to be held back.

"We can start by calling the police station and getting a list of who's been arrested."

"You think he's going to be arrested?"

"I think an Indian boy's on the top of their list, Elisabeth."

"So what do we do?"

"Bail him out, if he's not dead."

The rest of the ride is quiet. We make good time because no one is driving that direction. WLS has stopped their rock music and now is carrying continuous news warning us about a "state of emergency." About that, they are right; Chicago is a state of emergency.

My heart is in a state of emergency, too. *Bail him out if . . . if . . . he's not dead.* They have killed one Indian boy already. They could easily kill another, and it could be Anaquad. Out loud, I say what I am thinking. "I should have gone with him."

"You think that would have stopped anything from happening, Elisabeth? Don't fool yourself."

I am hesitant to say more, sensing that my father and I are moving into a land that we stay purposefully away from. I go ahead anyway. "Dad, I look white. I feel white. If I were there, a white girl . . . it might be different."

He says nothing, but he looks unbelievably sad. "You do look white, Elisabeth," my father speaks quietly. He turns down the radio and I strain to listen. "But if you think your looking white would stop these police, you're naïve."

"Dad, it might be different if I were there. . . ." I continue.

"Yeah, you'd be a white girl in jail with a bunch of half-breeds and full-bloods. You're right, they probably wouldn't kill you, but they could make you watch them hurt your boyfriend right in front of you."

"Why are you saying this?"

"I'm sorry. I don't know. I raised you white, but I don't want you to be stupid and get hurt." I am getting frustrated with him. He always seems so rational, choosing the best option. White is safe, but I'm not sure I want safe anymore.

"So you raised me white because you thought it would be safer for me."

"It is safer, Elisabeth."

"I don't think so. Anaquad thinks I'm a complete coward."

"Doesn't surprise me."

I am hurt again. "Why did you say that?"

"Elisabeth, I'm sorry. I wanted you to be safe. Maybe I think I'm the coward. Look, you're no coward . . . you're here."

Yeah, I am here, but that doesn't mean I'm not petrified. I notice police blockades ahead, so I swerve to make a sharp turn and exit the expressway. The city's streets are deserted. No police, no pedestrians, no one at all. Dad dispatches directions calmly. "A right two blocks up, left at the underpass." But I notice that the sweat running off his hands is smudging the ink on the faded street map. His relaxed attitude is a front; he is scared, too. What are we doing here? He keeps giving me directions and I keep driving until we park in a deserted lot on Lower Wacker at the edge of the river.

Nearly invisible at dusk, the river is recognizable by its offensive smell of rotting garbage. Ignoring the staggering heat and humidity, Dad puts on and buttons his top-coat, pulls out his pocket comb and slicks back his hair, angling his summer straw hat with the plaid band on his head. He hands me the comb, inspecting my peasant blouse and skirt. He hands me one of my mother's cardigan sweaters from the back of the Plymouth and waits while I put it on before he links his arm through mine. Just a father and a daughter on a summer night stroll. We follow the river for a couple blocks, passing groups of teenagers, running. I can hear a screeching whistle from the elevated train above us. Finally Dad stops and points.

"Wells Street is up there, Elisabeth. I think that's where the shooting happened. He told you he was there, right? I'll go up and check. . . . stay here."

"Dad, I think we should stay together." I'm not sure whom I am more worried about . . . him or me.

"Okay, but if we get stopped by the police, let me talk to them. If we get separated, you know where my office is. There's a watchman on the ground floor, usually sleeping, but not tonight. Have him open my office for you."

Trailing behind him as we leave the river and walk toward Wells, I stumble on the damp stone stairway, slimy with moss, and reach for his arm again. We aren't going to be separated.

The streets have a deranged carnival atmosphere, deserted of cars. Groups of people, even adults in suits with convention badges, are running quickly through the streets. Though just past dusk, it seems very dark, a darkness that is broken only by sudden flashes of light. Dad silently points to broken streetlights. We wait, hidden behind a parked car, until most of the people are gone, and then step into Wells Street. Looking left, I can see searchlights flooding several blocks away.

Dad speaks softly. "That's where they shot him, Elisabeth."

Together, Dad and I stand in the middle of Wells Street. I feel close to him, even more than when we linked arms at the river.

"I'm glad you came with me, Dad."

"So am I," he answers.

We start walking toward the lights.

"What do you think is down there?"

"I don't know."

"You . . . don't think Anaquad is dead?"

"No, I don't, Elisabeth."

I can hear him breathing. We are close now, only two blocks away. Still no people. I keep staring ahead at a gray mist, growing thicker now, a cloud gliding toward us, hanging above us, below the stars.

Raaataa taaa Raaataa taa. Sharp noises . . . maybe gunshots? The cloud is slowly sinking, blanketing us. More noises . . . stomping . . . marching . . . then I see them, a wall of uniformed men . . . soldiers . . . police. Their faces are hidden by visored masks. They are moving toward us. In slow motion, Dad is turning toward me. I feel like I am underwater—dreaming.

"Elisabeth, get down low! It's tear gas—cover your face!"

The last thing I see before I pull Mom's sweater over my eyes is Dad hooding his face under his seersucker jacket, his straw hat bouncing into the street, rolling toward the moving line of people. The fog has descended, bringing a thousand needles with it . . . pain. My bare shoulders and neck are burning.

Eyes blinded, I feel my Dad's arms around me again, this time pushing me to the curb. I trip against it but he pulls me up. Then we are running. We cannot see, but we are running very fast.

The Meeting

I awake from the dream-feeling on the floor of Dad's office, in a pool of water. Dad and Warren, the night watchman, are holding the water cooler over my head. My arms and chest are now burning, afire with throbbing red blisters that are spreading under my skin. The night watchman pulls out extra uniforms for Dad and me to wear, as our clothes are contaminated with poison. I change in the office bathroom, afraid to look in the mirror and see if the gas has burned my face. I open the window of the bathroom and push my head out, hoping that the night air will soothe my stinging skin. Dad's office overlooks the stinking Chicago river. Some twenty floors up, I am now too high to smell it, but I can hear police sirens and see sudden flashes of light. Anaquad is out there somewhere . . . I know it.

When I return to the office, Dad is talking to Anaquad's father on the phone. I can tell by his tone—steady, even, his baritone voice softening to reassure—that Anaquad's dad is drunk.

"Looks like we're on our own with this, Elisabeth," he says when he hangs up.

"No surprise there," I answer disgustedly.

"Most dads wouldn't want to get involved in this kind of thing. I wasn't exactly eager, myself." He smiles.

"Yeah, I had to hijack you."

He and I are talking to Mom, who wants us home immediately, when Warren appears with three oversized Oscar Meyer hot dogs with the works, Dad's favorite, chili and onions on the side for my benefit. We calm Mom and start calling the nearby police precincts. Warren seems to know someone at every front desk and describes Anaquad and his friends as his overzealous nephews. "You know how kids are . . . they want a little action."

To me, action is the very last thing that I want tonight, and I know it isn't on the mind of Anaquad and the others, but this story seems the quickest way to get information. The office is so quiet that I can hear the voice on the other end of the line as Warren holds the phone.

"Did your nephews know that the National Guard had been called out . . . not just the riot control division of the police? Did they know that the police were fully armed and shot off a thousand canisters of tear gas and pepper spray? Warren, you had better stay in your building, because the gas is drifting over Chicago. Yeah, a bunch have been arrested, a lot of 'em have been clubbed. Do we know about any juveniles? Well, they weren't asked their ages when they were dragged in. The 9th precinct is being used as a holding pen. That's probably your best bet."

The 9th precinct night sergeant says he will send over a police car to pick up Dad and Warren. As he puts it, "No sane person should be out on the street tonight—only crazy kids, conventioneers, and police."

"I do not want to be driven to the station in a cop car. What if Anaquad sees me?"

"Elisabeth, you're coming to bail him out of jail. He should be happy to see you any way you get there. And remember, you don't have to go."

"I'm going."

Several minutes later, the three of us get in the rear seat cage and thank our chauffeurs, who seem about as scared as we are. "These kids in the National Guard are seventeen. They've never shot a weapon. They're dangerous," says one of the policemen. The ride to the 9th precinct takes a very long time because the police drive slowly, radioing their precinct constantly. They offer to wait for us while we look. Apparently, this assignment is safer than some of the alternatives. Dad accepts their offer.

Inside the station, we can see that we are not the only ones seeking someone that evening. The 9th precinct lobby is flooded—Chicago citizens of all ages, clothed in makeshift head and eye gear, their exposed skin covered with angry burns, dazed conventioneers with watering eyes and skewed badges of patriotic red, white, and blue, riot-garbed soldiers with gas masks hiding their faces, anxious, searching friends and relatives—and the entire scene being chronicled by reporters holding smashed cameras.

I scan the faces. . . . No sign of Anaquad anywhere. I want to leave, but feel myself being pulled by Dad and Warren through the crowd. Locked doors are opening and swinging shut behind us. We struggle to keep up with the policeman, scurrying through dark underground corridors. A stench . . . the river again . . . fluorescent light, and then we see it, the holding cell of the 9th.

A crowd of shouting, armed police, wearing hooded masks, are hosing down twenty or thirty half-naked, shivering men. They are huddled together, waist high in rust-colored water in the flooded pit, struggling to avoid the spray on their blistered skin. One man is separated from the others. Nearly covered with water, he floats on his back, bleeding from a hidden wound that colors the water around him deep red. The guards are targeting him with their hoses—watching his head bob as the water hits it—making a game out of trying to make him sink. When a heavy stream pushes him completely underneath the water, the guards laughed so hard that their hooded visors fly back and reveal their faces. Unable to look at the tortured men, I stare at the guards who are laughing so hard they are choking.

"Stop it! You'll kill him!" My father's voice is louder than I have ever heard it. He yells again, "What are you doing? You will kill this man!"

The police do not look at my father, but they stop laughing and spraying the drowning man. I force myself to look and see that another man is now kneeling in the bloody water, holding the other man's head in his lap. He moves the tortured man's face close, and I hear him speaking quietly to him. This voice I recognize as Anaquad's. I also see that his face is bleeding, but I notice that his eyes blink when my father speaks.

The room is suddenly very quiet. The hoses have been turned off. Everyone is watching Anaquad cradle the body of the drowning, bleeding man. It is my father who moves next. I see him enter the holding pen after he gets the guard to open the locked gate. One . . . two . . . three . . . together, they work to breathe the dying man back to life.

Bloody water spills from his mouth. I find myself beside them, kneeling in the water. We lift him up. I'm not sure . . . is this Anaquad's cousin? I can see that he is Indian, but I don't recognize him. His face is swollen and deep purple. He was hit hard before he fell in the water.

Anaquad and two of the other prisoners place the boy on a stretcher and carry him out of the cell. The police follow but do not touch us. My father and the guard who took us there walk ahead of the others. I follow with Warren. We leave the holding cell of the 9th and walk up the stairs, circling through corridors, until we are again at the front desk. No one speaks. It is completely silent, except for the metal doors opening and closing. An ambulance is called and the man is carried into it. The medics place a rubber pump over his mouth and continue the breathing. They drive away.

I touch the bloody cut on Anaquad's face, but we don't speak. He acts as if I am a stranger and he is living in a world that I am not part of.

Different Kinds of Dying

All of us are different after that night in Chicago. During the days that follow, I sneak in on the train to the Democratic Convention and see others gassed, clubbed, and beaten by the police and National Guard. Anaquad joins me some of the time but mostly sleeps outside his cousin's Intensive Care room at Cook County.

Months later, the Walker Report calls the Chicago Convention the worst example of a police riot that has ever occurred in America. I watch the trial of the Chicago 7, the so-called leaders of the demonstrations, on television. They never once mention the shooting of Dean Johnson, the Sioux boy whose death sparked it all. My senior year begins a month later and I apply to the University of Wisconsin. After that night I can stand up and march with the others, and I'm not afraid on the outside—inside, however, I am terrified. I cannot forget what I saw that night. I want to fight back, but I know that I cannot kill people and that makes me feel weak. My dad and Anaquad—they are the strong ones. I forget that it was my idea to drive to Chicago. I remember instead the twisted pale faces of the Chicago police as they sprayed the boy and hate the part of me that is white.

After that night, Anaquad changes, too. He bares a three-inch ivory and purple scar on the side of his right cheekbone and wears a black bandanna on his arm to commemorate Dean Johnson. He begins to talk about Indians joining together to fight back.

"If we don't, they'll kill us all, just like the buffalo. You too, Elisabeth. You'll be wearing that armband with the native stars, your

Choepi, just like the rest of us. Half-breeds will die with the others. It'll be like it was with the Jews . . . Auschwitz in Illinois."

He starts going to meetings as far away as the Dakotas where other young Indians gather and talk. I go a few times, but I can't seem to listen. It's not the Indian part. I'm beginning to get a better grip on that and see that I'm neither Indian nor White, and I'm not exactly like my Dad or Mom, at least not in the way they handle that part. Anaquad keeps calling me *Mixed-blood*, maybe to reassure himself that I've got at least some Indian part. What really bothers me about the meetings is that they are always talking about shooting and dying.

I also know that Anaquad now keeps a rifle under his bed. On nights when we sneak into one of our bedrooms, he wakes up, his arm shaking, stuttering, *"We've got to save him . . . breathe . . . one, two, three. . . ."* His mind still spends the nights in the holding pen of the 9th precinct. I stop wanting to sleep with him. Both the rifle and the way he thinks scare me.

I miss him a lot, at least the way he used to be, and I suggest we go out to Herrick's Lake and watch the shooting stars, but before we go, he insists on putting his rifle in the backseat. It makes him feel safe. He says, "You know they want to kill us, Elisabeth. Other kids have to go to Vietnam to die. Indians they kill right here on Wells Street." He is right. The Anaquad that I knew was killed that night in the holding pit. They may as well have sent his body to the Chicago morgue with Dean's and Anaquad's cousin's. I wait out my senior year, thinking, "I'll leave in a few months." But I never stop thinking about him. Do you give up on love and sex when you find out the world can be a terrible place? Not me. I think about it more than ever; I just stop doing it with Anaquad.

Dad is also different. He has always been a man who chooses his words carefully. He still does that but just chooses different words now, and uses a lot more of them. In a letter he writes to the Chicago Tribune, he tells the story of what he saw that night—the tear gassing and drowning in the holding pit. He talks about the death of the Indian boy,

Dean Johnson, and even mentions Anaquad. He says that he is ashamed
of his city, our city. He signs it "A Half-Breed Attorney from Chicago,"
using his real name, Gilles Beaucoeur. After that he tries to spend more
time with Anaquad, sometimes accompanying him to AIMS meetings,
but mostly he talks to him and tries to get Anaquad to talk back.

One night, Dad tells Anaquad and me about his grandfather, Louie
Riel. The way Dad tells it, Riel was a mixed-blood who was more white
than Dad or even me. But as for his spirit—white, Indian, and Métis—
Riel's was free. Anaquad has never heard about Riel before but he is
really interested. Dad gives him a book of Riel's writing and Anaquad
asks me to translate the political papers into English for him. I am more
interested in Riel's poetry and read those on my own. After this, Dad
tells me more about Angeline, describing how she is like me. She tried to
save things, too . . . her songs, her stories, her *médecine*. Dad thinks she
was the strong one, not Riel. But I realize that, at this point, Dad believes
that saving things is what is most important. He saved himself. From
this perspective, his marriage to my mother makes a lot of sense. Her
sharp mind and dogged perseverance are definitely survivor traits. Her
criticism of me, and sometimes even of him, is part of that roadmap. At
least she is looking out for herself. She won't die. Dad and I both know
that a lot of Indians die.

Watching all of this, I think of the spring day that the ice broke,
when Dad shouted to us, "Save yourself." Skate, swim, run . . . take a risk
and stay alive. This is what he had done, and he believes it is how he has
survived. Save yourself. But how does that fit in with saving others? After
this, I am making that choice. It is the Chicago night which gave me the
idea to study medicine. If we had known what to do in that pit, maybe we
could have saved that boy. Although I don't wake up to nightmares, I live
mine and never stop thinking about that drowning boy.

After I become a doctor, I see his face masked over those that I
bring back to life. For me, every one of them is an Indian boy with dark
purple bruises, and I save him over and over again.

Choice

*A*fter that summer, I single-mindedly hold to my goal of medical school, racing to complete my university studies by the end of my nineteenth year. Dad helps me organize my applications, only once questioning if I should take it a bit slower. This is after a conversation that we have about Anaquad working too hard for the Indian movement. He wonders if I'm not doing the same thing with medicine. But I am sure that I have life figured out. It's simple—I will save myself by saving others. They will live; I will live. No one will have to die.

I ride that passion hard until the end of my first year when I am placed in a summer externship in the emergency room of Cook County. I have the night shift—midnight to sunrise—the busiest hours, filled with beautiful broken bodies of teenagers who have just received their driver's licenses, street toughs who cut each other open with beer bottles and then explode their wounds with bullets, and coding business men suffering heart attacks, still wearing their jackets and neck ties. We save some, but others die. And I watch it over and over. That summer, I don't leave the hospital much, sleeping in the on-call room for medical students in the back of the emergency room. I scavenge for food on the warming tables of the hospital cafeteria on my four am breaks. But I am usually too nauseated by what I've seen to be able to eat much.

On one of those breaks, late in the summer, Anaquad walks into that emergency room. I haven't seen him in years—the stories that I hear about him scare me off. No calls, no letters, no contact until one night. Dad tells him where I work. Anaquad sits on one of the plastic and metal folding chairs for four hours waiting for my shift to end. I leave with him. We walk across Chicago to the lake, lay on the sandy beach of Michigan, and stare at the morning sky. We don't talk much; he has just spent hours seeing my world and I'm not sure I want to ask about his. He is still into politics—Indian politics. That doesn't surprise me. He is no longer using drugs—that does surprise me because I had no idea he was using in the first place. I try to be cool about it. Everyone I know in college uses something and will continue in medical school, just better quality drugs. But it's hard to believe that he does after he has tried so hard not to be like his drunken father.

We sleep together during that summer of surprises. It is different from the summer of shooting stars—no kisses, few touches—but we need each other even more than we did then. We are still teenagers. He is nineteen and I am turning twenty but we are being sucked into an adult world.

At the end of the summer, he leaves for South Dakota where Indian leaders are gathering, and I begin my second year of medical school. For me, school is a relief. No one dies in lecture halls or libraries. This time, he promises to write.

Snow is falling on the Chicago beaches when I realize my body is changing. I send my own urine for the pregnancy test and call the laboratory for the results. I telephone Anaquad first, unsure about what I want to say. Do I want him to come to Chicago? Marry me? Do I want a baby? What about medical school? Conversations follow. Somewhere in the middle of these discussions I realize that Anaquad doesn't want to tell me to abort the baby, but he will not be able to be a father to the child. It is my decision and my responsibility. I try to talk to my mother, but once she hears I'm pregnant, and obviously unmarried, there is no talking, and in her mind no choice. She doesn't have to say it. I remember all too well the "homes" for unwed mothers that my high school girlfriends lived in and left without their babies. I'm not going to be sent there.

The winter that follows is a dark one. I vomit between my classes, and comfort myself by wrapping my face in scarves and my body in oversized coats—a disguise no one recognizes as I walk the shores of Lake Michigan. Dad and Marc help a lot. No ice skating—Dad cooks and Marc paints my apartment.

Beginning in late February, Anaquad and a group of Indian activists join the Oglala Sioux and barricade themselves into the South Dakota town, Wounded Knee, to form the Oglala Nation. Over three hundred national guardsman and U.S. marshals surround the village and wait. I follow what is happening in the *Chicago Trib*, although Anaquad calls me when he can sneak out and access a phone. Our future becomes clearer. He is going to stay there. And I am going to have a baby.

Anaquad and the other Indian leaders are at Wounded Knee for 71 days. They finally agree to leave the village in exchange for promised talks with the government about how the Indians are being badly treated. Two weeks after they agree to leave, they receive a letter from President Nixon informing them that the days of treaty-making with the American Indians ended in 1871, 102 years earlier.

My daughter, Anne Beaucoeur, is born in a Chicago hospital several days later. Dad sits by my bed as I stare at my baby's face trying to decide what to do. My mother visits but tries to convince me to give Anne up to "a good Catholic family" for adoption. I look at her small pink cheeks, a little rosebud, my baby. I still haven't told anyone at the medical school that I was pregnant. Dad is clear about two things: he believes that I should keep Annie, as he nicknames my new baby, and adds that, in his opinion, I don't need to get married—ever. I agree with him about the keeping Annie part, remembering that I made that choice while walking the shores of Michigan during the winter. At first, I don't understand why he is so adamant about the marriage part. Maybe my mother's Catholic legacy has rubbed off on me a little bit. I feel like I need at least to consider marriage, notwithstanding Anaquad's lack of interest.

The way dad sees it, it is fine—better than fine—to have one committed parent. Fathers who are pressed into paternal service through blood, guilt, or duty give their children an undesirable legacy—one that he doesn't want for Annie. Anaquad's choice is just that—Anaquad's choice.

And my choice is also mine. After I come to my decision, Dad talks about Angeline. Like me, she loved a man who had another passion. And like me, she conceived a child with him. But then she made a choice to marry a man that she did not have a passion for. Dad doesn't say how that choice affected her or him, or even his father, Joe, but I know that it is a legacy he doesn't want for me.

Although Dad mentions neither the passions nor politics of Riel or Anaquad, I think about them a lot. I believe that all Indians and half-breeds have to stand up, even when the outcome is certain defeat. But what I really want to ask Riel and Anaquad is, "Are these causes that are worth dying for enough compensation for missed lives with Angeline and me?"

Annie

My Lodge

this will be my lodge
skin stretched tight over bone

this I will call my home
sacred place I cannot leave

no light visits me
in this womb
thick with hot, stone-breath

moonlight beats
in the ear of the world

stars wonder
where I have gone

my soft voice centered
rises
and
falls
with the wind

—Randy Lundy, poet of the Barren Lands First Nation

The Healing Journey

Mom has always told me that 'Medicine' is a great word in her country, the land of doctors. For her I think it is holy, a sacrament, even though it is peddled by drug companies that make millions. Grandpa tells me that the Métis also believe that it is a sacred word. In their language, a healer or doctor is called a *médecin*. The Métis *médecins* are all reportedly magicians, skilled in the mysteries of healing. They carry their *médecine* with them just like my mom carries her prescriptions today. We are leaving for Medicine Lake.

I'm driving, not because I want to, but because I have more room that way—I don't have to be crammed into the backseat. Grandpa sits next to me while Marc and Mom argue in the back, wedged between the camping stove, sleeping bags, and cartons of food. What did Mom pack in the trunk? And where will we stop for breakfast? They've already started discussing it. No camp stove yet. A truck stop with eggs-over-easy or a bakery with scones and lattés? Why is it such a big deal, anyway? It's early, and the sun is rising. Who needs to eat? Grandpa and I both put on our sunglasses just before we drive onto the Golden Gate Bridge. The sunlight fills our overstuffed car as the first rays hit the water. This bridge glows. I drive slowly, not because I don't want to get a ticket—I just want to see the light on the water. I look to fiery Mount Diablo in the east as the sun pops up behind it, casting a copper light on this land of water and islands engulfed in the morning fog. My English teacher says we San Franciscans live in Avalon, a mythical place of misted islands and foamy seas, and this morning I finally see it. San Francisco. A Magic

Kingdom. I try not to get into an accident, but look long enough to freeze this image for a future photo.

My teacher is right. I need to be on this trip.

As we pull off the shining bridge and wind up the steep road leading into Marin County, I break a promise to myself and look back. I want to see it— the hot, glowing bridge wrapped in copper fog, leading to my city. Bad luck. My friends are always telling me, "Don't turn around, Annie. You'll be okay. Just don't look back." Of course, they aren't driving their sick grandfather and half-crazed mother and uncle into the wilderness on some kind of pilgrimage road trip. They don't have this kind of family. With this family, you look back. My friends are in school studying, or at least they will be in a few hours. And I'm here.

We have one rule in my family that I completely agree with. If they hadn't come up with it before I was born, I would have insisted upon it. The driver controls the radio, and everyone must go along with it. It is still early—B.C., Before Coffee—so I don't want to torture them yet. We can start easy with the morning news. Grandpa says we need to listen to the traffic report. That should take about ten seconds. We are headed north—against traffic, I remind him. He is worried that we will run into some in San Rafael . . . no, not likely, a few cars maybe. He reminds me that there are other drivers on the road at seven in the morning. But traffic? I think Grandpa just wants to drive. Then I see it—they are already shouting directions from the backseat and we have only driven a few miles—everyone in this car really wants to drive. They are just letting me because I'm the youngest, and then they can feel kinda supportive . . . keeps their caustic comments to a minimum.

Passing Petaluma in well under an hour, there really is no traffic. Then a scream, "Lay off, Marc!" and I realize we are going to have to stop. Mom and Marc are going at it in the backseat. Are they really adults? They need their coffee now. I pull off just in time. Grandpa is intervening. "If you two can't agree, we'll get coffee in a gas station. You can just pour the milk into it, Elisabeth. I don't see what difference it makes."

He likes his coffee straight up. Like me. We can drink our coffee anywhere.

"Look, Dad, you used to drink it with milk in it. I'm like Mom. I like milk, only I have to have a little foam in it." Mom sounds pleading for so early in the morning. Funny what coffee jitters will do to you.

"Elisabeth," says Marc, "I'm sure that we can find that in a truck stop. After all, this is your country—California." Marc has a one-track mind, too. He wants eggs, potatoes, and bacon.

"My country is San Francisco . . . land of lattés. Truck stops use machines to make theirs. I want a person to make mine." Mom is even firmer now.

"Well, I want to eat at a place where they have real food, not just scones. Those things are crumbly. They break all apart and the part that you eat tastes like sawdust." Marc pretends to spit, but tactically backs off. "Choose your place. I just won't eat."

"Black coffee for everyone. First gas station we see, then we're back on the road," intones Grandpa.

Now, even I know that this is not the greatest idea. These people need to eat, or even being able to control the music is not going to make a difference. . . . This trip is going to be real hell.

In small families like mine, every person makes a big difference. With Mom and me, when one person leaves, half the family is gone, but it seems like a lot more. And now this thing with Grandpa that I try not to think about. We all try not to think about it, but are we really thinking about anything else? I stop myself here. . . . "Concentrate on the driving, Annie," I tell myself. I need coffee desperately now. I turn off 101 and then I see it—a tacky grey shingled building with a peeling latté sign and a lot crammed with semis. It looks like someone tacked a kitchen onto the back of a house. That'll work. Truck stop for Marc, lattés for Mom.

Clutching our coffee, Mom and I go to the bathroom together. She starts jabbing at her hair, twisting it into a mound of furry fuzz and piling it on top of her head. I tell her it looks okay, even though it could use more brushing. Mom is fastidious about her appearance, but when she is under stress her hair is the first thing to go. I want to talk to her, tell her that I think she has done a good thing to bring her dad here to visit after we found out about the AIDS. I want to tell her that it's going to be okay, even though I'm not sure. But I don't. I coil her hair into a smooth twist—think silk, Mom, not fuzz—and refasten the clumsy barrette at the bottom of her neck. "There, Mom."

Breakfast is predictable. Marc eats double portions of eggs, sausage, bacon, and ham; Mom discusses his rising cholesterol; Grandpa devours the map; and I, too, am calmer with coffee, recognizing that I'm probably getting my period and it is not just this crazy family trip that's irritating. The Humboldt County Jail is our first destination so that Mom can do the evaluation of that Indian kid, not exactly California's foremost spa, but Marc is more than game. He is a lot better after breakfast. Grandpa says we'll camp on the coast, a rocky inlet south of Eureka, leaving us only a morning drive to Humboldt.

Jail

Surrounded by long-branched drooping redwoods raining mist, the Juvenile division of the Humboldt County Jail appears protected. Mom and I walk into it together. Once inside, even this illusion of safety is gone. Three sets of bolted steel doors must be crossed before we are inside. At the first checkpoint, we are met by a stooped Indian woman leaning on a carved oak branch. She is Mary Johnson, the tribal leader of the Wigots and the paternal grandmother of Sarah, the girl who Mom is going to interview. She is looking past Mom, searching for someone through the small glass pane in the metal door that is slamming shut behind me.

"Have you brought your daughter, Doctor? Sarah will not talk with you unless Anne is with you." Mom pauses and the woman speaks again. "Annie, your daughter, the filmmaker."

I step out from behind Mom and say, "I'm Annie."

Mom doesn't seem to want me to go inside. She mentions that they probably won't let a child in. Mary motions, nodding ahead to a group of young faces clustered at a window. "There you are wrong, Doctor. That's all they let in here . . . children."

Later, Grandpa reminds Mom that I'm not the first teenager in our family to visit a jail.

After Mom finally agrees that I can join, she and I walk into a long corridor lined with rooms guarded by metal doors and tiny wire-mesh grates. From behind the grates I can see girls' faces peering at me. Mary stops at the last door where there is no face. Our large guard, a woman I guess, fumbles with the lock and I see Sarah sitting on the bed. Like me, she has long red-brown hair and gray eyes with yellow rims. She looks scared. I reach out my hand and say, "Hi, I'm Annie. Nice to meet you." It's not that I usually do this kind of stuff, but it seems like the right thing to do. Sarah takes my hand, shakes it, and holds it before she finally lets go. Mom asks if we'll be okay together. Looking into Sarah's eyes again, I know we'll be fine. Mine also look green in the night. Mary gives Sarah a kiss and smiles at me before she and Mom walk out. The guard asks for my purse, stuffs it under her arm, and tells me that she'll be right outside, before she slams the door shut. Sarah makes room for me on the cot next to her. There is no space for a chair.

I don't know what to say to her . . . that's how I end up reading it . . . her poetry. Sarah just kinda dumps it in my lap . . . "Here." Shit, this girl can write. It is all here—running away from home at twelve with some twenty-nine-year-old guy after her dad dies. Then she goes back to take care of her little brothers and sisters, after her mom is sent to a place for druggies, and then her stepdad rapes her and now she's in jail for killing him. From her telling it, killing him was the best part of her life, so far. I try to think about what is the best part of mine, and I just can't. Maybe it's because there just haven't been any real bad parts to compare it with. My AIDS test was negative. Grandpa's wasn't.

I mention to Sarah that I take my journal with me everywhere. Sarah asks if she can read it—I have never shared it with anyone, but I ask the guard to get it out of my purse and I give it to her. For a long time we just sit there, each of us turning pages. . . . It is better than talking. One of her poems is about being an Indian—she thinks it is part of the reason that they put her in jail. "They wouldn't do it to a white girl, would they? Just us 'cause we're Indian." She half-smiles at me. She says *Indian*, not *part-Indian*, not *half Indian*, not *a quarter Indian*, but just *Indian*. She thinks we are alike, at least, some part of us.

I believe her about the jail stuff. I know from my mom that they put Indian kids in prison for things that they wouldn't even arrest white kids for, like running away. Sarah is in jail for murder, but it's different if it's self-defense. Of course, Sarah won't say that it is self-defense. In fact, she says the opposite. She tells me she wanted to kill the bastard. Her stepdad earned it. She's got it all worked out. Her sugary attorney keeps trying to get her to say that she was fighting him off or trying to protect her little sisters, so they wouldn't be raped. "That wasn't it," she says. "He deserved to die."

"I agree with you," I say. He raped her. For me and her, it's simple. Her attorney told her that if she says that they'll give her seven years. Maybe she'll get off with three and a half if she is lucky. It's funny, I start wondering about her junior prom. Do they have dances in jail? Hell, I'm not even planning to go to mine. Nobody goes in San Francisco.

Up until now, Sarah has been quietly reading my stuff. Then I see she keeps returning to one page. No, it's not my poems. I realize it is my list of film ideas. I see that she is trying to ask me something.

"Would you ever make a film about someone like me?"

"A girl like you?"

"Yeah, a half-breed girl who gets raped by her drunk stepdad and then kills him. She's no pity case, this girl," she starts to plot it out.

No pity case. Just what does she think about me? "Sarah, I don't think you're a pity case. . . ."

"So, would I be your heroine?"

"Maybe. I'd want to tell your story. You tell me—are you a heroine?"

"Sometimes I am. I don't want to be a victim, just another Indian victim."

"That's not how I see you."

"Why did you come up here?"

Why did I come up here? Because my mom made me. Because my grandfather is dying. Should I tell her about AIDS and the Medicine Lake business? Probably not, after her stuff about not being a victim. Do

I think Grandpa is a victim? "I came with my family. But I'm different from you . . . I don't exactly have it worked out."

"And you think I do?"

"You seem to. I think you were right to kill the guy."

"And now I'm in jail, for a long fucking time. You've worked it out better than I have. You can maybe make your films. I'll be in jail."

What can I say to her? I look down at her worn sheaf of poems that I'm still holding. "Look, Sarah, you can do this—you can tell your story. I feel the heat of the iron lampstand before you crack it over your stepfather's skull. I see the ugly sparkle in his eyes before you break the light. I taste his tongue pushing into the back of your throat. Sarah, you can do this even in prison."

She takes her poems from me, and I think she smiles but turns her face away real fast. Her voice is husky as she grunts, "You're a cheerleader, Annie, just like your mom." She catches me off guard—no teenage girl wants to be told that she's like her mom, especially at the moment she might be. And a cheerleader—who does she think I am?

"Okay, so maybe I am a *cheerleader*," I exaggerate the word, gesturing quotation marks with my hands, "and I sort of need one, otherwise my films will never be made. You need one, too, or you'll never leave here, neither will your poems. We Indian girls don't want to end up pity cases." I am surprised at myself as these words roll off my tongue—a thrill and also shock of fear at the embrace of *We Indian girls*.

"Should I lie like my attorney says and call it 'self-defense'?"

"You think saying that makes you a pity case?"

She nodded. "Yeah, I do."

"Then don't say it." I have a question for her, too. "Sarah, why did you want to see me?"

"My grandma told me you were a filmmaker-storyteller, a mixed-blood girl. . . . I don't know, I guess I was looking for someone like me to talk to."

"Who would understand?"

"More like, help me understand. I don't have it all worked out, either."

I leave that jail feeling like I've got a life sentence, too. I feel like I have to prove that Indians have a voice. I've got to make up for all the ruined lives—the silent Indians, the missing ones. And I've got to tell their stories, all of them.

Creation Myth

*T*he day has been really long. Mom says her interview with Sarah was testy. She questions whether she should have let me talk with her, although, I tell her, Sarah and I really opened up with each other and it probably helped Mom's interview. I wonder why I'm so tired. Am I down? Maybe thinking about Grandpa, Sarah, too. Most of the time I'm so high-energy, but tonight life seems so hopeless, even impossible.

We are sitting at Mary's house. We have just finished picking clean the bones of the smoked river salmon whose naked skeletons now decorate our plates. I'm encircled by Grandpa's arms, my legs stretched north toward the oak fire. My red-brown hair is catching its dancing light, spilling into Grandpa's lap when Mary begins her story. Three of Mary's puppies are scuffling at the fire's edge, a squirmy pile of shoulders and legs tussling over a shadow. Her grandchildren, Sarah's younger brothers and sisters, are clustered at Mary's feet. Mom stands near Mary. Only Marc is standing on the edge of the circle, deciding whether to join the others. I breathe deeply, close my eyes, and when I open them, he is gone and she has begun.

Mary is an old-school type storyteller, not like me. We're similar in one way: we're both edgy, just hanging onto different edges. She's a looking-back type, I want to catch this moment, tell what's happening right now. My camera does it for me. Mary's different, grabbing for the past, her voice starts off kind of screechy—eeeeiioo—like she was pulling her story out of the ground, but then it rises, mellows into a smooth flow. Grandpa's eyes are tightly closed, but I can feel his head nodding up and down, following Mary's voice. Everyone is listening.

"My grandfather was an elder of the Ahjumawi clan, one of the Pit River people, and it was he who told me this story." Then she pauses, eyes still shut, and draws a half-circle on her closest grandchild's palm. Opening her eyes, she stares right at me. At that moment, I feel like she has moved inside my body. What is happening? I know her words even before she says them. And this is how I want to write them for my films, sensing them even before they are spoken.

"In the land of the Pit River people, God lives on top of a mountain that breathes fire, but is covered with ice. It is on this peak that the creation of all things takes place. Rock people, plant people, animal people, my people, and our family were all given life there. The Creator enjoys giving life, and after spreading His energy, He comes down from the mountain to share himself directly, and bring His spirit to the world. With Him, He brings His only son, and together, they stop and look at everything He has created. Then, They swim and bathe in a great lake at the bottom of this mountain, joining the water that shares the spirit fire of the earth. They swim for hours, cleanse themselves, and then the Creator's son climbs to the surrounding mountains to pray. The Creator looks again at the world He has created. From the shores of the lake, He sees far, observing the world that He has made and recognizing how much evil and suffering exist. He cannot abide this evil, and decides that He wants to leave the world. So He soars back into the sky. However, His son stays in the hills near the lake, searching and praying. God is now alone in the heavens. He cannot forget the earth or its people.

"High on the mountain, He looks down and feels sorry for the earth and those that He has created, so He decides to help them and give them a gift—His spirit. He sends His spirit to the earth, to the lake where He swam with His son, and it is there that his Spirit remains. When you swim in that lake, you connect with the spirit of the Creator. But it is not the same for everyone. Some follow the path of the Creator's son and go up into the mountains to pray, and they, too, connect with their power.

There are things to fear. When we can no longer swim there and join with the Father and the Son in the lake-waters, the world will be overcome with evil. This is the lake that you are traveling to. This is the story of Medicine Lake."

[faded text]

Swimming

*H*ow much did Grandpa know about Medicine Lake? I sense that he has heard Mary's story even before she tells us. Is this why he chose the lake as our destination? Or is it coincidence? I can see that Mom is right when she says that he is "a man of purpose whose life is defined by actions." Never a talker, not like Mary or me. Yet he communicates his thoughts clearly with others. Mom says he is similar to his grandfather, Riel. Both cared about the lives of others and took risks with their own. But I know that they are also different. Riel left Angeline and Grandpa has stayed with us, at least until now.

We're in the car again, headed for Medicine Lake. It is the largest volcano in California. Grandpa insists that I read the forest service brochure from the Trinity Alps Ranger Station out loud. I read, "A volcano bigger than Shasta or Lassen, but hidden deep inside the earth." Medicine Lake, Mary's site of power, is a caldera, an underground volcano. You can't see anything. We're driving past Shasta now, a place with icy slopes and clouds wrapped in clouds. This is where I thought Grandpa was taking us. I can feel the power of this mountain from fifty miles away. Sitting in the backseat with Mom, I am the first to see it, a sharp snowy mountain standing alone, carved from clouds. If I wanted to camp, Shasta is the place I'd go. If I had a spirit, this is where I'd feel it, but this is not where we're going. We've still got a couple more hours to drive.

Last night at Mary's home, after the others had fallen asleep, and she and I were cleaning up after dinner, she told me another Ahjumawi story. I was scraping the fish bones into a fertilizer can when I decided to ask her about Sarah. Ever since we had gone to the jail, and I'd met her granddaughter, I couldn't stop thinking—this girl, just two years older than me, is spending years of her life in prison. While Mary is calmly making dinner and entertaining us with these amazing stories, her granddaughter is locked in a jail cell, receiving food on a metal tray. I saw the staff passing it out—no salmon, wild mushrooms, and certainly, none of Mary's fry bread. How can Mary stand what is happening to Sarah? I blurt it out. I sense that she expects it, because she answers immediately, scraping as she speaks.

"My granddaughter is like you, Annie. She has a strong *tinihowi* (guardian spirit) protecting her, even in that scary place. When she was ten she asked to go to the mountains and search for her spirit, so I took her to Shasta, and she camped there alone overnight. When she came down from the mountain, she was protected. Her spirit is with her now, even in jail, guiding her."

"I want to go to Shasta, too. Do you think I have a guardian spirit like that, Mary? What about my family?"

Why do I ask her that? I don't believe in this stuff—*tinihowis*—they make nice stories, but then great storytellers always have nice stories. But, this isn't just some story. I want to believe that there is some spirit for Grandpa. And for me. And it feels like Mary knows.

As if she reads my mind, she answers, "Your mom's *tinihowi* is different than yours. She is a medicine woman, and gets her spirit from a *tamakomi* (strong spirit) coming from the medicine itself—but it can also suck the life out of her. That kind of spirit either cures or poisons people. Your mom needs to fight her spirit or it will consume her."

"And Grandpa?"

"I'm not sure about your grandpa. But I know he has a spirit. Go with him to Medicine Lake."

"Well, I don't have any choice. I have to go."

"There you are wrong, Annie. You always have a choice."

Why do I say that to Mary? Don't I always tell my friends that we have choices? I know it—we are the ones who have to make things happen. No one else is going to do it for us; I argue this with my friends all the time.

I tell them we have control if we take control. My friends agree with me, or at least when we were in elementary school they did. After we got to high school, and started thinking about boys, things changed for them. It's because they're not just thinking about boys—they are obsessing over them. Joanna forgot that she wanted to make music videos. All she talks about is her boyfriend, Max, playing his guitar. When I ask her about her own stuff now, she just shrugs. Maya's held on better than the others. She tells me that she is attracted to girls. I think that kind of forces her to take control. But now she is starting this diet because she thinks she is too fat. I like to believe that we have control over our lives, but sometimes it is real hard to see. And I don't tell them what I'm really worried about—that someday we won't have control, like that night on Larkin Street when a group of guys messed with Maya and me, just because we drank some wine with them. I'm never going to give up control again. You give it away, let it seep out of you, and it doesn't come back. I'm going to keep control of my life. No one is going to take it from me either, and I sure am not going to give it away.

So why do I tell Mary that I don't have control?

Later that night I lie next to my mom, unable to sleep. I can't stop thinking—nonstop films play in my brain theatre. Another loss of control? At first, I want to fight it, turn off the projector, but it's an automatic digital, always running. After a while, since I don't feel like I have control; I lie back and watch. That's when I notice that I am the actor in only about half of these films. No glamour queen either. In one, I'm eating dinner. Don't know what it is, but it's served on a metal tray. No surprise, I'm living out Sarah's life. In the others, I am doing everything, writing the script, directing the action, working behind the camera, and cutting in the editing room. These films seem more real. Waking up early,

I wonder if I'm some sort of control freak. I need to run my life and my dreams. I don't want to stay in bed anymore.

Searching for coffee, I head for the kitchen and discover Mary standing at the oven heating oil for pancakes. She hands me a cup of coffee, and I tell her, "Mary, I do have control over my life. I don't know why I told you I didn't."

Smiling, she hands me a knife and points to a pile of apples. "If that's settled, Annie, cut these."

Her knife is sharp, but the apples are wormy and I have to concentrate to avoid slicing my fingers. To save them, I postpone future discussions about the meaning of life. We work together silently frying apple pancakes until there is a mountain of them stored in the warming oven. Mary pours me another cup of coffee (mine got cold while I was helping her). Instead of discussing my theories about control, I start talking about Sarah killing her stepfather. She listens. When I've said everything that I can think of, she asks, "What about your Dad, Annie?"

Just when I thought that I had control, she goes and asks me a question like that. Even thinking about my father makes me feel out of control. What do I say now?

Silence.

Fathers are a quiet part of my story. My father is not really quiet. (I've seen him a couple times, so I know that.) But he has never said much to me, and do I care? Yes, a lot. It is not lost on me that a lot of kids with problems have absent fathers. Sarah told me that her real Dad is dead. She said she never thinks about him, but I don't believe her. Some nights my Dad lives in my dreams. Mom has told me some things about him, like he used to ride a motorcycle, and that he fought at Wounded Knee, as if these two random events are connected. She doesn't blame him for not being part of my life. But I do. I still haven't answered his last letter.

The next morning it takes us two hours to drive from Shasta to Medicine Lake. Just because they're connected underground doesn't mean that it's easy to travel between them. As we jump off of Interstate 5 and head into the wilderness, Uncle Marc insists that we stop for provisions in McCloud, a half-deserted logging town. He reminds us that we will be gone more than a week.

I walk into the McCloud convenience store with Mom but after looking at the California fast food wonders—organic hohos, microwavable burritos—decide that there's nothing for me and leave. Not a problem—I know Mom loaded the car up with organic food. When I come out, Grandpa is sitting on the edge of the wooden curb on Main Street, resting his boots in the dust. Several feet off the ground, the wooden sidewalk makes a comfortable seat for both of us to watch the road, an unpaved dirt wonder about four times the width of any street in San Francisco.

"Imagine, Annie, that they used to drag huge logs up here—oak, cedar, pine, even redwood—moving them abreast through the dirt to that train station at the end of the street. This isn't a street for walking."

I try to imagine it, but my family is the only thing here now—no trees, no loggers—just us and the guy at the convenience store who winks at me and smiles when he tells me that they sometimes have tourists up here and that there's lots of deserted boarding houses to stay in. Tourists . . . hmmm . . . this sure isn't one of those times.

Uncle Marc exits the store and stands in the road, stretching his six-foot frame. He tells me he's going to walk these streets. As he heads for the train station, joking about it being an historical tourist site, he mentions that we should savor this last memory of civilization. Is he saying this for my benefit or Grandpa's? This is not a place I would want to come back to.

Sitting there, Grandpa asks about my dreams. This question is not a surprise. Other families ask how you feel, how you've slept, what you're doing that day. Mine asks about dreams. I want to talk with grandpa about my nighttime movie theatre and this control thing, but instead, I start telling him about the jail dream. Locked doors, metal plates, cold food. . . . He doesn't say anything but his head is cocked, eyes staring straight ahead and I see he is listening—really listening. When I finish, he still doesn't say anything. After a few minutes, I mutter, "Whatever," under my breath.

Very quietly, he says, "Annie, it has to be your dream. Your film. It has to be your dream."

"This is my dream."

"The frontrunner?" I want to tell him about the others, but Uncle Marc is back at the curb. So I don't.

"We all have our dreams, Annie. When Angeline was about your age, she dreamt she would ride in a buffalo hunt."

Now I really don't say anything. The buffalo hunt story stops everything. I've heard it from Mom, when she put her feminist spin on life. "Girls can be doctors. Hey Annie, they can even chase buffalo." The way Mom tells it, it seems a whole lot easier to be a doctor than chase buffalo. Buffalo were always the pinnacle. Now, Grandpa.

Pissed, I answer quickly, "There are no more buffalo to chase, Grandpa."

He laughs, his voice echoing on the empty street. "There are always buffalo."

Mom shouts from the door of the convenience store, "Hey you guys, table the buffalo talk and help me carry these groceries." Just what has the organic food queen bought in there and why doesn't she ask that winking guy to carry it for her? Once I'm in the store being looked at by him, I understand and pick-up five gallons of water and ten pounds of potatoes without protest. Where do these guys come from? Then it occurs to me if they're at the last outpost of civilization, they're everywhere. Point for wilderness camping is to get away from leering men.

We are all quiet during the last part of the drive to Medicine Lake. Oso Butte Cinder Cone and Pumice Stone Mountain remind us that we are in a volcanic area. Marc wants to take the scenic and longer route circling the Ice River Caves, but the rest of us vote against it. Grandpa's eyes are closing, his head nodding against my shoulder as Mom pulls into the final turn on Modoc Volcanic Highway.

The broken surface of Little Glass Mountain reflects the late afternoon sun sparking light flashes. The road twists open, and we see the lake. It is not beautiful. The volcanic landscape that frames its shores is full of spare-stunted pines and sparse branches robbed of the red-gold leaves that we saw earlier. The campgrounds are directly in front of us, and Mom pulls in slowly, parking in full view of the lake. No one else is here, just my family. We sit looking at the lake for quite a while.

Eventually, Mom gets out of the car and walks around to the trunk. I know what she is thinking: feed them, their energy will return. Marc joins her, and they begin to rustle in grocery bags, unpack boxes, and wrap potatoes in foil. Grandpa and I are appointed to start the fire, and we search the shore for dry tinder. Grandpa is moving very slowly, his eyes fixed on the lake. "I'm tired, Annie. You're going to be building most of this fire."

"That's okay." I am tired, too—exhausted—but I believe that he needs my energy now, and I struggle to hold on to it. When he stumbles, I see AIDS. I just can't get it out of my mind.

Together, we pile dry twigs, lifting the heavy oak logs from under the backseat and stack a pyramid. I watch Grandpa closely. I hand him a box of matches, and he lights the fire and holds out his hands for warmth. We are both thinking it. AIDS again—what do I say to him now? How does he live with it? How does he live knowing that he has it?

Grandpa is looking at me now, and even though his shoulders are sagging, and he's stooping slightly, his mind seems more alert. "So what are you thinking, Annie girl?" My eyes sting, tears shut them for me. "The AIDS thing?" he asks.

I nod. We stare at the lake. "I don't want you to die or suffer."

He nods and reaches for my hand.

"Don't you have some story for this one, Grandpa?"

"A story?"

"Yeah, like Angeline and the buffalo, or Mom and Wolf River."

"I don't have a story for this one, Annie." Then I see—no story, no map here. He is making this one up as he goes along.

It is dark when we finally fall asleep in the tents that Marc put up, after drinking hot tea and eating turkey sandwiches that mom makes.

The sun rises early the next morning, and we all dive into the water together. Marc is the fastest swimmer, the first to arrive at the far side of the lake. He is the first out, and I follow. From my granite seat at the lake's edge, I look up at scarred hills cut by lava, dotted with lodge pole pines. Sun-sharpened obsidian knives cut through jet flows as they reflect the early morning light. The Indians chose this place well. Pain is captured here. I shiver and worry that it will take me over. Jumping up, I throw myself back into the water, stretching out my arms. Down, down, down. In this dark water I see nothing. But the pain comes with me. Finally, I stop and realize that I will never reach the bottom. It does not stop. I turn and move upward headfirst, slowly surfacing. I imagine myself in the future, looking back—what will be there? Grandpa is a brown speck now, having turned and begun swimming back to the shore. He strokes right, then left. Mom is swimming with him, matching her movements with his. Finally, she splits off, dives, surfaces, and paddles back to us. Next to me, she turns and stares at Grandpa. She is not going to join him nor stop him. He is borne quickly by the currents. He appears to be flying—arms outstretched, silver-black hair flowing through shafts of blue light. He swims and we watch.

Spirit Dance

Mom once told me that the Cree search the night sky for their lost spirits. Mom dove to the bottom of Medicine Lake looking for Grandpa's. Mom says that modern medicine saves the body, not the spirit. The Northern Lights are not visible in San Francisco but I sometimes feel Grandpa's spirit in the water when I'm swimming with Mom. When I tell her this, she tells me that he is reminding us to save ourselves. After Grandpa is gone, I write a letter to my Dad and tell him that I need him to be part of my life. A couple of weeks later, I get a letter from a Sioux reservation on the Canadian border where he is living. He tells me that he would like to have me visit during my next school break. And I'm planning to go.

It is at Medicine Lake that I recognize that Grandpa is dying. But I don't accept it. Even now I haven't accepted it, but I know that it has happened. I don't believe in the spirits, the *Choepi*, but sometimes when I'm in the film-editing room—a dark cubicle where narrow frames of light and life captured on celluloid fly by me—I feel them. I remember Grandpa saying, "You must ride with the buffalo, Annie." And I think about what I now know—that before you can do this you have to search them out and find them.

I know now why Grandpa wanted us to go on that road trip. Indians used to get strong chasing buffalo; now we gain strength when we're chasing those spirits that everyone else has forgotten, those connections that others have lost, forgotten myths buried at places like Medicine Lake. I also see the film that I will make about that trip to the lake. In this one I am both the actor and the director. It'll capture those dream images locked in my imagination just beyond reach. I will find the buffalo, and this time it will be my story.

I spend a lot of time thinking about my last talk with Grandpa. My friends don't have those conversations with their family. They laugh when I say that my Grandpa is in the spirit world, dancing with the stars. But I know I'm the lucky one. If we can no longer ride with the buffalo, we have to search for someone who knows their story and is willing to share it with us. I want to be one of those people.

Author Notes

*E*ach of the four adolescents in this novel relates historical and cultural events which take place during their youth. Angeline describes the development of the Métis people as a political group in Canada. She portrays their struggle for self-government and hints at the attacks which follow their election of representatives. In 1869 during her fifteenth summer, the British-controlled Ottawa government destroyed the Métis effort.

Angeline's grandson, Gilles, describes his choice of Chicago street-life in the 1920s where he is threatened with incarceration in a reservation school or life in the French-Indian colony in Illinois. A generation later in 1968, Gilles's daughter, Elisabeth, describes her participation in events surrounding the Chicago Democratic Convention. Lastly, Elisabeth's daughter, Anne, describes her family's efforts to assist Native American youth in the 1980s and a visit to Medicine Lake, a sacred site of Native American people.

Angeline

Angeline's mother is a member of the Cree, the largest Native tribe in Canada. They are of Algonquin heritage and closely related to their southern neighbors, the Ojibwa, who gave them the name Cristino, which was then shortened to Cree. Until confined to reservations, they occupied extensive territory in the Canadian provinces of Manitoba, Assinibaia, and Saskatchewan. They believe that all living beings in the world possess a spirit and that the Northern Lights, the Aurora Borealis, are the dancing spirits of dead relatives. Most believe that death occurs only in body and that the dead join the ancestors who continue to share their spirit with living beings.

Angeline's father was a Métis, a mixed-blood of French, Cree, and Assiniboin heritage. The Métis culture developed in the 18th and 19th centuries in what are now the central and western parts of Canada. The group was a cultural mélange of French and Scottish hunters with Cree, Assiniboine, Ojibwa, and Saulteaux women. This culture included a distinct language, called Métis or Michif, a diverse economy, and a unique lifestyle and philosophy. Not surprisingly, Métis were tolerant of other racial groups. Many were risk-takers of a physical nature, a trait encouraged by the harsh geographical conditions in which they lived. Love of music and dancing, especially "jigging," a mixture of French two-step and Cree and Ojibwa dancing, was common. The Métis tradition of exercising, even their horses, to the music of the jig may have inspired the Royal Canadian Mounted Police Musical Ride, a dance with horses.

The Métis were also well known for their skill with languages. Many spoke Michif, French, English, and a number of Native dialects. They were widely used as interpreters. Métis or Michif integrates plains-Cree with French and is spoken in at least two versions, one described as "plain," the other as "fancy." A key philosophical value involved their perspective on raising their youth. Educating and sharing responsibility and equality with youth is an important social value of the Métis. Elders act as mentors and guides for young people and encourage them to take risks.

Louie Riel was the elected leader of the Métis at a very significant point in their history, 1858. For approximately a year, he led an elected assembly in Red River, Manitoba. In Canada, much has been written about his life, whereas in the United States and throughout the rest of the world, little is known about him. In 1869, he was exiled from Canada by the Ottawa government after the Métis government was overthrown.

He fled to the United States along with other Métis. He secretly returned to Canada several times and in the 1870s led a number of Métis in a bid for self-government in Alberta. As I describe, he was caught, tried for treason, and hung in 1885. He is buried in Red River, Canada.

Gilles

Gilles's story begins in 1927 with a journey by train to the French Indian Colony in Western Illinois, where his grandparents live. In this section, I have tried to accurately relate many aspects of Métis culture in the United States.

The Métis people of Canada and the French-Indians of the Midwest share many similarities. Both groups initially developed as a result of unions between French fur traders and Native women. These relationships are frequently described as existing between powerless, passive Indian women and French fathers driven by passion. Their progeny, the mixed-bloods, often derogatorily referred to as "half-breeds" or "bad-bloods," were believed to have acquired the worst traits of each race, including ignorance, alcoholism, and unmitigated risk-taking.

Dr. Thorne, in her extensively researched volume, *The Many Hands of My Relations*, counters these myths with well-substantiated descriptions of romantic and economic unions where mixed-blood individuals, both men and women, fulfilled the role of middleman in fur, agricultural, and liquor trade for generations. She reveals how they established strong family networks that influenced political and economic change in their geographic areas.

One difference between the Métis in Canada and the French-Indian mixed-bloods in Illinois is that in the late 19th and early 20th centuries mixed-bloods in the U.S. were "encouraged" to attend Native American schools (as revealed in Gilles's story) and to move to Native American reservations "for their own good." In Canada, natives were sent to reservations, but their mixed-blood relatives were not allowed to accompany them. The Métis in Canada continue to fight for rights, currently related to fishing and hunting, and access to reservations.

Elisabeth

Elisabeth's junior year in high school, 1968, was a year of extreme political unrest in the United States. In January of that year, the government launched the single largest offensive, employing a total of 542,000 troops in Vietnam. On April 4th, Martin Luther King Jr. was assassinated and on June 5th, Senator Robert Kennedy. Following this, the Democratic Convention took place in Chicago in August. After riots following Martin Luther King Jr.'s death, Chicago's Mayor, Richard Daley, gave the police specific instructions "to shoot to kill any arsonist and to shoot to maim or cripple anyone looting."

On Thursday August 22nd, the first day of the Chicago convention, Dean Johnson, a seventeen-year-old Sioux Indian from South Dakota was shot and killed by the Chicago police on Wells Street. A memorial march was held that evening.

Days of unrest and protesting followed. Political demonstrators were clubbed, beaten, and maced by the Chicago police. At a September 9th press conference following convention week, in a now famous slip-of-the-tongue, Chicago Mayor Richard Daley described the policeman's role: "The policeman isn't there to create disorder; the policeman is there to preserve disorder." The Walker Report, released in December of 1968, and based on a Chicago study team's evaluation of statements from more than 3000 witnesses, 180 hours of film, and 12,000 photographs, termed the events of Chicago during the convention week "a police riot" and identified how "spontaneous acts of aggression by individual police officers were responsible for the violence on the streets."

Although the Sioux boy Dean Johnson's death is referred to in Dean Biobaum's online chronology of the events in Chicago, his memory and place in history have largely been forgotten. Three months after his death, the American Indian Movement (AIM) developed by urban-experienced youth was founded in Minneapolis as a self-defense organization. In this section I have recounted many memories of that frightening summer evening.

Annie

On the way to Medicine Lake, Annie and her mother meet with a mixed-blood adolescent, Sarah, who has been arrested for a violent crime. Sarah is fictional, but her story parallels that of many girls.

Statistics from the U.S. Bureau of Justice report that Native Americans are imprisoned at a rate of almost 40 percent higher than the national average. Rates of violent victimization for both men and women are also higher among Native Americans than all other races. The rates of violent crime experienced by Native American women are nearly 50 percent higher than that experienced by black men. There are no comparable statistics for mixed-bloods. It is difficult for Native American and mixed-blood youth, especially girls such as Sarah, to obtain the type of medical and psychological evaluations and care that they need to prevent both victimization and unfair incarceration. Sarah's story is one of many and reveals the importance of conducting evaluations which take psychological and cultural factors into account, and provide help for Native youth.

Following the evaluation of Sarah, Annie and her family travel to Medicine Lake. The waters of Medicine Lake are embedded in a volcanic basin more than a million years old. Within a startling landscape made up of the largest collection of lava tubes and caves in North America and surrounded by obsidian mountains covered with hemlock, this lake provides a home for eagles and other wildlife. For more than ten thousand years, the Medicine Lake Highlands have been the site of native spiritual and cultural practices. The Native American peoples called the Ahjumauri (Pit River), Modac, Shasta, Klamuth, Karok, Wintu, and other more distant tribes have visited this area and believe that it is a sacred place.

The story of the Creation told by Sarah's grandmother, a tribal leader, reveals the power that many native people find here. Historically, many tribes have joined together to worship at Medicine Lake. It has been a place of unity. Today, many native peoples are united in a struggle to protect Medicine Lake from damaging development, most recently geothermal projects. In 1999, the entire Medicine Lake caldera was designated a traditional cultural district by the National Register of Historic Places, but the cultural and environmental threats have continued, including the destruction of spiritual sites and construction of power plants.

For centuries, Medicine Lake has united Native Peoples. It is with this spirit that I chose Medicine Lake as the destination for Gilles's last journey with his family. The Métis understand the importance of coming together as a family and value the importance of spirituality for all people.